Brown Glass Windows

a novel by

devorah major

CURBSTONE PRESS

FIRST EDITION, 2002

Printed in Canada on acid-free paper by

Best Book/Transcontinental Printing

Cover design: Stone Graphics

This book was published with the support of Charlotte Loomis Heaton, the Connecticut Commission on the Arts, and donations from many individuals. We are very grateful for this support.

Library of Congress Cataloging-in-Publication Data

Major, Devorah, 1952-
Brown glass windows / by Devorah Major. — 1st ed.
p. cm.
ISBN 1-880684-87-X (pbk. : alk. paper)
1. San Francisco (Calif.)—Fiction. 2. African American families—Fiction. I. Title.
PS3563.A3915 B76 2002
813'.54—dc21

2002000996

published by
CURBSTONE PRESS 321 Jackson Street Willimantic, CT 06226
phone: (860) 423-5110 e-mail: info@curbstone.org
www.curbstone.org

Acknowledgments

I wrote this book alone, and yet with so much help. I must give my sincere thanks to my mother and father, who provided valuable feedback and asked important questions. Thanks also to The San Francisco African American Historical and Cultural Society whose monographs provided information on the early Blacks in San Francisco. Thanks to so many of my neighbors of the Western Addition who just in telling me stories provided a thought, or historical perspective, that shaped the work. Thank you to Rex Griffin, Ezra, and Horace Coleman, whose insights into their Viet Nam experiences helped me be true to that part of the story. Thanks to Margaret Block who gave me a funeral story and asked me to put it in a book. And thanks to Alexander Taylor and Judy Doyle of Curbstone Press who believed that this book should get out.

The poem "fillmo'e street woman" was previously published in *street smarts* (Curbstone Press,1997). The poem "brown lady in white" was previously published in *Obsidian III: Literature in the African Diaspora* (Vol 1 No 1, Spring/Summer 1999). The poem "the bones, white, are fed..." is an excerpt from "death and ritual" previously published in *traveling women* (Jukebox Press, 1989).

Brown Glass Windows

1. Brown Lady in White

have you seen her?

she is shadows of africa buried
in a mausoleum of whiteness.
her gingerbread skin cracks through
the white paint
she brushes over her cheeks
across her forehead
down her neck
to meet a blouse of white
a long white skirt
white stockings
white sneakers
a white cape blanketing
away cold and rain mists.
she walks engulfed by white
cutting the air so quickly
that when she passes
she is often unseen.

i have seen her
clipping down mission street
gusting through the tenderloin
pushing past crowds on market.
a friend swears
she has seen her in harlem
and another claims
to have caught a glimpse
of her in the downtown of atlanta.

have you seen her
is she one of many?

she cannot become

the whiteness
she wraps around herself.
her skin tones break through
proclaiming color
"brown," they insist
"when we were young," they sing
as they rise above the paint
"when we were younger
we glowed in many browns
remember when?"

she argues with her shadow
speaks sharply into her collar
cuts the air with aspersions.
her steps are short and clipped as she
flies down the street
a whirl of discord
brown still
under the white.

have you seen her
walking faster and faster
until she almost disappears
shining brown
under the layers of white?

Victoria doesn't even remember her own birth year. I mean not exactly. She stopped counting birthdays over sixty years ago, when she first began her journey towards invisibility. But on the morning when this story begins, on that warm October day, before Victoria had her morning bath or anything, she announced to the mirror, just as proper as could be, that she was going to the ocean, and that I could go or stay as I pleased. Now, this is a woman who spends as much time in 1890 as she does in 1980, so as far as she's concerned most days there's no way to get out to the ocean besides a carriage.

Victoria is frail, but at the same time she's full of iron. People think she's a wispy sort, but that's a façade. The woman will crack your teeth with her resolve if you try and turn her from what she wants. But I tell you, when she said she was off to the beach, I could of lost all the kink in my curls. Well, of course I mean if I still had curls and kinks.

Now I know all kinda ways to reach the ocean, which buses and what street cars, all of that, but then I been here since even before the city's opening, when it wasn't no golden and wasn't no gate. It was almost like home then, I tell you. Ocean Beach was all full of life. You couldn't walk on the beach's edge low tide for all the presents the ocean washed up, not just broke-off pieces of jelly fish, ropes of kelp, and cracked sand dollars. Yeah, I know every stretch of sand and water on this peninsula and knew the best way for Victoria to get to the beach. But she starts out striding fast and mumbling under her breath right past the nearest bus stop, like she was going to walk those miles to the beach.

There was no way she would have made it on foot, so I directed her towards the bus. Of course she took offense, telling me she knew "perfectly well how to get to the beach, without your help." Well, knowing doesn't mean doing, that's what I always say. Folks know all kind of stuff. Far as I can see, more often than not, it doesn't make a bit of difference in the doing.

Well, anyway, we got on the bus and rode all the way out. Then we walked over to the beach, and off went Victoria to the water while I just hovered on the sidewalk, taking a moment to feel the ocean reaching up to make the horizon curve. By the time I caught up with Victoria, she had taken off her shoes and stockings and was sitting on the edge of the shore, legs outstretched, with the waves licking all between her toes, just watching the bubbles dissolve, happy as you please, sitting still as can be, so won't nobody but me see her.

Of course, I know other folks see her, especially the children, but I got to give it to her, she's almost as invisible as me. I don't think too many folks with a body can get any closer. Not a whole lot of folks can get to it like she does, but then, not a whole lot of folks spend most of their life aiming to just disappear. But like I said, some see her no matter what she does. Like when we just got settled in right on a corner of the shore, a little freckle-faced boy, couldn't a been more than four, five years old, he was holding a pail with one hand and pulling on his mama's leg with the other, asking, "Why's that old lady all painted up in white? Is she going to a Halloween party?" Of course the mother had only a half an ear to her child, and just kept moving, hardly noticing her child twisting around. "Is she a ghost, Mama?" the child kept asking, pulling on the woman's pant leg.

But his mama—well, she was busy watching a gull swoop down and dip its long beak into the water and try and get himself a nice little rock cod for lunch. "Look, Sammy, see how the bird just dives under the waves—when he comes up he'll have a fish in that beak," the mother called out to the child.

"But Mama, Mama, is she dead?" The mother didn't even

turn around to see what he was looking at, just kept talking to her son. "They don't have dead people sitting on the beach, honey. You have such an imagination." And the little boy, he kept screwing his little self around his mother's arm and staring at Victoria, who just kept watching the little bubbles of salt burst around her ankles. Victoria didn't see the child see her; so far as Victoria was concerned, and matter of fact, far as most everybody else was concerned, at that moment she was invisible.

Victoria was full of a moment of contentment like I hadn't seen inside of her in quite a few years. It was as if she had just finished with one important project and was getting ready to start another. Now, since she doesn't do much of anything sides the day-to-day work of living in her basement rooms and going out to get the different free meals they offer at this shelter or that, or go shopping at a thrift for some white gloves or white skirt or white something, there really is nothing that she ever, properly speaking, accomplishes. In fact, even the shopping isn't real "shopping." That is to say, most times she just kind of slips whatever it is on top of, or underneath, what she's already wearing and leaves the store. Sometimes though, for gloves and handkerchiefs especially, she lets herself be seen by the saleslady just long enough for them to bring out the tray from the back room, or from under the counter. But before that clerk has time to sneeze, or I have time to say "Bless you," Victoria makes herself thin and flat and quiet, and they forget all about her and go help another customer, or answer a phone, or just start daydreaming about what they really would like to be doing. By then Victoria is always down the street with her new pair of pearl-studded gloves, or a soft white linen handkerchief. Now Victoria certainly doesn't think of herself as a thief. Her feeling is that once clothes have been bought and paid for, they were bought and paid for. A body isn't supposed to be selling and reselling the same pair of gloves, or crocheted doily, or camisole.

But then there I go, wandering down the wrong alley again, that's what Victoria always calls it when I start yammering on. I was telling you about us being on the beach, wasn't I? Now, I can't say I remember but one other day that she ever went to the beach, at least since I've been around her, and that was the day after they laid her mother under. Of course most everyone could still see her, but by then, most folks didn't care to look. She just wasn't the sort that you noticed in a room full of people, or for that matter a half-empty room neither. But today, why she's just washing her feet in that sea water, and just sighing in the sun. It's been so long since I've seen Victoria really smile that I just don't know what to do. I know one thing though, soon as she realizes folks is seeing her she'll be bustling back to the middle of town where she's safe. Still, I can see that the ocean is giving her a healing. There's some things only the ocean can fix. It's been here before, and it'll be here after. It knows all the stories, and has buried about as much as it's birthed, so it carries a kind of peace inside it.

Victoria says she came out to the ocean to hear it cry, says that's all the ocean knows how to do, mourn the passings. Mourn and get angry. But Victoria's a foolish old woman. I've been with her since she was hardly more than a girl, and she's been foolish ever since I've known her. Of course, that's why I decided to try to bring her back around. I needed to give myself something to do. But Victoria, she never wanted my kind of knowing. And me, I guess I just didn't want to believe I couldn't make her see. I've been here so long, you'd think I'd a made more progress. But no. She been stuck on this turning invisible idea since she was hardly a girl of twenty, and now, well, she's edging up to the end of her eighth cycle, and funny style as she is, I wouldn't be surprised if she made it to her dream of turning into light without giving up her body. I still don't have a clue as to why she wants to do that, though. If I could of held onto my body a little while longer, you know I surely would have.

Me, when I had body, I glowed shiny like some polished ebony. Sweat was the stars, and my back was the sky spread out, when I danced at the harvest festivals. Before I passed over, or tell you the truth got stuck, I was already promised to be married. My mother was teaching me my part in the ceremonies for that day. I was to marry Kueleza. It was decided by others, but only after it was already clear that we were bound in the spirit, through the heart. We had danced together, he in the outer circle, and me in the middle. We had danced together, and we knew that we were fated to have children, but then the sickness took me. Before we had even one night together, the sickness came on me, and my body died, before I ever had a chance to feel him up inside me and have our babies grow. But one year after my death he put on the mask draped in a long cloth. I could tell it was him by his toes, the second one was too long, and curved like a spoon around the large one. And I knew because when he danced it was just like me. It was like all that watching me, year after year, made him know me in a certain way, and he called me back, called me to come join him for one last dance. And I did. I spun with him and tried to fit my toes on top of him, and hold onto his back so when the sweat started streaming from his chest it ran down my breasts too. But after the dance was over, he took off the mask and never danced for me again. I was supposed to go the other way with all the other maidens who had been danced for that day. But I decided to stay.

See at the dance I noticed that I was still full of all these eggs, just thousands of them that could never be turned to children. I died with all those eggs up inside me, all those eggs ripe and wanting to become. I can't remember how I found out I could do it, but somehow instead of just moving on like I was supposed to do, I started eating the eggs one at a time, pulling them into me from my flattened ovaries, so that my spirit force could keep seeing and moving and dancing.

At first, I didn't know what to do. I followed Kueleza

around. He knew how to work with iron. He met travelers at the market, sometimes traded with them. He had a gift of tongues and soon knew words in French and Portuguese and a few in English. I told him to be wary. But he would not speak to me. One day while traveling the day's walk back to our village, he was captured and pressed into service on a ship. I rode with him and watched him learn the seas and learn the strangers' ways. And everywhere we voyaged he learned languages until he became an interpreter.

I would try to speak to him. He never spoke back. But each time we landed in a new place, he would walk on the beach, scoop two handfuls of sand, and slowly let the grains sift to the ground. Then he would ask, "Will you stay here?" I never answered. Then one night I saw him jump the anchored ship and swim to the shore. I moved with him. When he reached land, he rested on the warm, damp sand and watched the waves wash over his feet. He stood and looked in my direction. It felt like he saw me, as if I almost had weight and substance. He did not speak to me. He walked through the space where I should have been, turned his back to the moon and sang, his feet sliding across the ground lifting lightly as he moved towards a dense inland forest. I did not follow. I came north instead.

That's what got me here all the way across the world to San Francisco. Of course, when I came, it wasn't San Francisco. It wasn't even Yerba Buena yet. When I came, it was just on the edge of becoming California, named off a story about some Angolan woman warriors who fought as well as men. I don't think I could leave this place now. I've tried, tried to leave here, tried to leave Victoria, but I can't move outside the city limits anymore. I wouldn't mind going home. I think I could have gone once, but now, seems like I'm tied to this place.

But now I've wandered on so, you've got to forgive me. Victoria is always chiding me about the way I chatter, but there wasn't anyone else to hear me speak for over two hundred years. That's a long time for a self to be seeing and thinking they knowing something, and don't have nobody to talk to, to check out things so you can make a judgment if you seeing them true, or getting caught into a mirage. Just being around a long time doesn't necessarily mean that you know all there is to know. It's amazing how long a body can get stuck in wrong thinking, I'm here to tell you. But now I was talking about Victoria, wasn't I?

Now Victoria's folks, they know she's alive. Sometimes her niece even sees her. But they all just kind of pretend she's never around. They go along with her invisible thing, since it means she doesn't bother them. And it's not hard to pretend, what with her keeping to herself so much of the time. I've been here the whole time, but I'm still not sure how Victoria does it. I mean she's just got this way of turning folks' eyes away from her so she's not seen. But there are some places she won't go, and one of them is to the beach. She says she doesn't go to the beach because she says when the sun starts to setting, folks can see her on the edge of the water's reflection. Ain't that a hoot, crazy old lady.

Victoria ain't but oh, five foot four and hardly a hundred pounds, so it's not like there's all that much to see. It takes her hours to get ready to go, with her having to pile on all those layers of white clothing, from inside to out. Then she's got to paint every last inch of uncovered skin till she's nothing more than some crumpled old writing paper blowing down the street. Not that her face is all that wrinkled, her neck is and her hands, but her face is kinda smooth, which is amazing, considering she been stopping it up all these decades with her paints and powders. That woman loves some white.

Well, after sitting still as can be for a couple of hours, all of a sudden like a gust of wind Victoria started moving and was pulling back on her stockings and slips on her shoes. Without even calling to me, she started walking towards the wall to see what these two young people were doing. The boy lives a few blocks from us, but I don't remember ever seeing the girl. These are teenagers, too old to just see Victoria right off, but then again their eyes are clear and sharp, so they just might. Especially that boy Jamal. He seems to be shielding the girl, so no one can see what she is doing. And the girl, why she is painting the most beautiful horses you've ever seen on the seawall. She was moving fast as can be, making these long strokes with her thick black marker. As I watched her draw, the mane started falling across the horse's thick straight neck, and the legs, they started lifting high like they are ready to fly off the wall. That horse was so bold and shiny black, you could almost hear it neigh. The girl was just laughing and painting; and the neighbor boy (we see him all the time painting his place into corners of the city), he was shielding her. He wasn't saying anything, just watching. Yeah, that Jamal was just hanging there, all tall and gangly, frowning, as usual. I tell you, the boy doesn't have his parts fitting together right yet, some parts too long, and others too skinny. He got this long head, and these little short pokey, what they call dreadlocks coming out.

Well, I was getting ready to turn to Victoria and ask her if she remembers that this is a neighborhood boy, Jamal, calls himself Sketch, when he looks her straight on in her eyes and says,

"What you think, ghost lady, girl got some skills, huh?"

Now usually Victoria, when she's seen, she just turns and hurry off so fast people think they was stuck in a daydream or something because when they look around she's gone. This time though, Victoria doesn't run or nothing; she just keeps her eyes on the boy and starts talking to me. "He got a light coming out his fingertips. He dark, but he got a light all coming in him."

"Yeah? Well, ghost lady, that's because I'm planning on lighting up a mess of walls." Well, that was it, that was entirely too much conversation. First of all, Victoria wasn't talking to him, she was talking to me. Second of all, Victoria hates rude people. So, just like that she took a spin and was gone. The boy didn't even see her go, and tell you the truth he didn't seem to care either. He just turned to the wall and started to drawing misshaped letters. At least that's what it seemed at first, but, as I watched, they turned into some sort of a stick. Victoria was way up the beach, but I didn't care. I wanted to see just what he was filling the wall with this time. As it turned out, each part of the stick was a letter, s-k-e-t-c and then he made the last letter "h" on its side and backwards so it came to a point and looked like the end of a paintbrush. Just needed a drop of paint coming from the end to be finished. That's what I thought.

I was kinda impressed too. I mean it takes something to push and pull all those letters and come up with a picture and a word at the same time. Well, Jamal started to reach out his pen again, and the young lady yelled out, "Sketch, 5-0 up the way," and the two of them took off running. That boy, he was like some kind of a gazelle pulling all those long knobby limbs under him, and about leaping up those stairs and across the highway into the park. Victoria meanwhile she stepped in front of the policeman just enough to slow him down a touch. I mean, he didn't see her, just hesitated like a wind pulled him back a taste.

I caught up with Victoria and asked her why she helped the boy. "Didn't do a thing, you old haint. Just getting out the way, that's all. Didn't do a thing." Then Victoria she did the strangest thing, I mean even strange to me. She walked right on back to the ocean and took her shoes back off, but not her stockings, and just stood there until the fog started to come in off the water. Everything was getting all gray and frosted, and she just stood there like she was home in her parlor looking out the window. Just every once in a while she'd say, "I have not seen a light like that in a long time. No, not in quite some time. Boy has a certain glow about him."

Then, she walked over to the wall. She asked me, "Do you think that after we leave, the horse leaps off of that wall and starts prancing around?" Of course I answered back, "Victoria you are as loony as they come. Let's go on home."

"Who are you calling loony? I really wish you'd mind your manners. I ask you a simple question requiring only a simple answer. I declare, you are so insufferably rude!" And then she didn't say a word to me the entire way home.

2. Tags and Pieces

crax *is everywhere*
store fronts, and bus stations
subway train ads and
city bus ends.
crax *is unrelenting.*
mist *retired when the swirl*
and corner of each marking
turned from love to addiction,
but **pure** *still rides the buses*
and counts on the schools.
while **sketch**
takes command
in the heavens
inscribes freeway overhangs
darkens billboard siding
crosses bridges and
laughs his paints around the bay.
he hangs from his knees
swings out like an acrobat
that no one ever sees
laying thick black strokes
proclaiming, "i am more
than you will ever see!"

Jamal "Sketch" Everman did not notice Victoria when she stepped in front of the policeman, causing him to slow down. He saw barely a flash of white as he leapt up the beach stairway and bounded across the sidewalk into the wide parking lot; he stuffed his pens into his bulky jacket pocket. Then he lifted one long arm into the air and pointed his middle finger at the sky, while jumping out of the way of an incoming car and heading toward the mouth of Golden Gate Park. He didn't turn around to see if a policeman was behind him. He knew he was not.

The officer had a thick waist and was wearing pounds of weaponry around his belt. He didn't have a chance against the speeding legs of this young new African.

Sketch loved to run. He was not all that excited about athletics. He had once humored his father by hitting baseballs across a field, and was still an adequate player at basketball, but running, well, that was his art. He could set a pace and cut through air like an oar slicing through water. Sketch spread across the soft pavement, as sweat began to roll off his head, down his neck, and cool the ridges of fear that had gripped his spine just moments before. He threw back his head, shook it, and laughed, free in the moment. There was nothing but the flat sour scent of dry eucalyptus leaves, and the algae sitting lightly on top of the duck pond. Sketch ran until his lungs began to ache and his thighs began to tremble. Then he folded over himself, and hung down his arms, scraping the ground, feeling the fog coming in behind him. After a few moments, Sketch stood up and started walking slowly down the sloping hill.

He took his time walking through the panhandle of the park over to Divisadero. As the street started to flatten out and he passed the busy traffic of Sutter Street he began to run again. Sketch could smell the fog thickening at his back. He felt the coming evening's chill and began to move through it.

A few blocks in back of Sketch, patrolling the boulevard in their just-washed police car, were Hank and Joe. They had moved some prostitutes from this corner to that one, given some tourists directions out of the hood, stopped a young man for speeding, and issued a couple of parking tickets. A nice quiet Friday afternoon. Joe was bored and glad to be bored. Hank, though, was enjoying intimidating drivers on the flat stretch of the long thoroughfare. Hank pulled up close next to the brown Chevy sedan with the dented left rear bumper, "Watch this, Joe."

He slowed down and looked at the driver, who had seen the patrol car in his side mirror and unconsciously straightened up just an inch. "See, man, watch him look at his speedometer and ease his foot off of the gas. You see that, man? I bet he's going to try and buy some ass, and is scared as shit we might pull him and find a violation. Sometimes, I swear to God, I just love being a cop. Man, there are these times, I just love it. I get hard when I drive down the street and cars slow down. People change lanes, people slip down in their seats or slump over just a bit or look harder straight ahead, and I just love it. They see me and make some kinda change.

"*Yes, sir*. That's what they call me, *sir,* even if we don't say a word. *Yes, officer, Mr. Policeman, Mr. Cop, Mr. Roller, Mr. Asshole.* Even when I got my knee up their back, and wrapping their elbow around my forearm, and they are sputtering shitballs in my direction, "Take away that badge and gun and what'd you be then, punk?" 'Punk, Sir,' I say. 'I got the badge, the gun, and just took my foot out of your ass to lay you on the ground. I'm Punk Sir to you.'

"The point is, I'm the cop. There are a whole lot more people taking orders from me than giving them to me, you understand? It's a pecking order and I got my place in it. I got somebody to peck. I peck, they squawk. That's how it works."

"Hank, they don't give a shit about me or you," Joe had started smirking in the middle of Hank's speech. "Those young bucks will shoot at us as soon as they'll spit, and they don't give a good goddamn who we are or how much fire power we got. They don't fear us, and they sure as hell don't respect us. We're nothing but some kind of a lackey as far as they are concerned."

"Oh, now they fear us, man. Look at this one, probably a family man coming home from banging one of those whores up around the corner. A little man who eats crap at work all day long, and then goes home to deliver some to the little woman. And lucky us, we get to serve him up a little more on his drive home. They care, man. They care. All of them change when we go by. They notice us."

"You're wrong as hell, man. Most these people don't give a damn. Some have fear inside of them, and some don't. You just have a knack for spotting the bluffers, but there are plenty with heart, a lot more than you or I probably want to admit."

"Why are you a cop if you think so much of these assholes?"

"Hey, I wasn't talking about regard. I'm just saying not everyone feels the way you think they do about cops."

"I ain't talking about all cops. I'm talking about me. See, I get my dues. I've busted plenty of head, and plenty of ass. When the judges forgot their job, well, I stayed on top of mine. I got the real power. It all starts with me, no bust, then no kinda trial and no kinda sentence. It starts with me. Maybe I don't make the collar, and there's no trial, but I still can make my point. Shitheads, a whole load of shitheads in this neighborhood. And cleaning up some of the shit starts with me. I'm the one who decides when we turn our heads and when we pounce, a card-carrying servant of the people. Yeah, I'm a servant of the people if they act right. And when they don't, I turn into the boss. Sure, some of them look at me with all that hate when they drive by. Some kind of glaze over and peek out the corners of their eyes, a few even laugh. But see, it doesn't matter how they look at me. The point is they look. People see me!

"Now you, you're alright. But Joe, you're just not quite as much a cop as I am. You just don't get the whole point of it. See you want people to smile and treat you like you're the same as them, but see, you're not. You're not the same as them. You're the same as me, and we're cops. We're different. Even a man in a Mercedes Benz has to pull over and get out spread if we tell him to. We might not have a whole lot of things, but one thing we have is power. People change when we come around. We could get them to change a lot more if cops like you would just come around and do what you know you need to do.

"See, your problem is that you don't like when it's fear or distrust people give us. I don't care, just as long as they know who I am. Give me mine, and you can think whatever the fuck you want. I'll take it easy or I'll take it hard. However you wanna give it to me. But I'm a cop, and you have to give me mine. I love being a cop. I fuckin' love it.

"Let's pull this one over, see if we can make him pee in his pants. I fuckin love it."

"Hank, let him go. Car looks clean and he's not breaking any laws."

"Registration was up last month."

"Hank, give him a break. Let's be glad we can just ride. I'm not feeling that good. Let's just ride and take it easy."

Hank shifted back in his seat, and eased down on the gas pedal, making his car slowly pass the low- riding Pontiac. In the block ahead, he noticed Sketch running. He was covered with sweat and moving quickly around the pedestrians. Hank turned on the siren, shot out in front of the boy, and pulled up into a driveway cutting him off. Neither Hank nor Joe saw it as harassment. They simply knew that the boy was too close to the upper-crust neighborhood of Pacific Heights to be running. They needed to know what he was running from, a person, a crime, or a confrontation. Hank jumped out of the driver's side, and threw himself in front of Sketch.

"You seem to be in a mighty big hurry, boy. Where's the fire?"

Sketch hurled out his reply, "Running ain't a crime. Why the hell you fuckin' with me?"

"Don't use that language with me, punk," the officer snarled back.

"Yo mama's the punk."

"Wasn't I just talking about assholes like him, Joe? You got any I.D., boy?"

"No."

"You in school?"

"Not right this second."

"Don't fuck with me, boy."

"I'd fuck with your mama, but the line's too long."

With that Hank grabbed Sketch and threw him to the ground. He twisted his arms back and placed a knee in the boy's spine while he placed on the plastic cuffs. "Give me a name."

"Jamal Everman"

"Jamal-Ever-shit-man." Hank laughed, turning to Joe, "Call it in. Sure thing this punk's on probation for something."

For the next five minutes no one spoke; then Joe returned, "He's got a vandalism jacket, but right now he's clean, according to the books." He went over and put his foot right in front of Sketch's face which was still pressed against the pavement. Hank leaned down almost spitting in Sketch's ear, "But we know better, don't we asshole?"

Joe stepped forward. "Let him up, man. We've got no reason to hold him, and we've got a long day today. You want to start out with all that paperwork?"

Hank stood Sketch up, yanking him by the shoulders. He cut off the plastic cuffs, "You're a lucky boy today." The young man's eyes were full of defiance, stomach cramping around itself; he was relieved that he wouldn't have to call his mother one more time to say he was in the hall. At least this time it wouldn't be for graffiti, but Mitch wouldn't believe that. No, Mitch would be talking about "What were you doing besides running, boy?" Like you had to do something to catch the rollers' eyes.

The officer patted Sketch down and confiscated the two thick-tipped pens he was carrying before letting him go. "You want to live a long time, I suggest you slow down."

Sketch started to open his mouth and then thought better of it and set his lips back close together.

"Get on out of here," Hank shot out at him as he got back into the car.

Hank leaned over to Joe, "The reason they don't respect you is you don't make them respect you. He's just lucky I'm feeling good today, or I'd a put my foot up his little bony ass."

Sketch turned and walked the long way around the block to get to his grandmother's house. On the way, he started seeing new ways to make a piece out of his tag name, he started planning new places to announce to the world that he existed, and to make it clear that he was planning on being around for a long time. Yeah, a long time drawing, and a long time running, not running from, but running to whatever he was running to, running to the corner, or running to his girlfriend's house, or running to feel good.

3. He Lives Drugs

he lives drugs
he lives drugs that
make his dreams swell
he lives drugs that make
his dreams swell, his pains diminish
he lives drugs that make his dreams
swell, pains diminish and his wife bitter
he lives drugs that make his dreams swell, his pain
diminish, his wife bitter and his children cry
he lives drugs that make his dreams swell,
his pains diminish, his wife bitter,
his children cry
and his wallet flatten
and his soul crumble
he lives drugs

Victoria and I rode that rattling streetcar back towards downtown and through the tunnel. I sat next to her and she got up and moved. I sat in back of her and she got up and moved. I swear that woman gets a notion and doesn't let go of it. Don't bother her with the facts, because when she's in a snit that's all there is to it. Finally we get off at the bus stop at the foot of Fillmore. Instead of transferring to the bus, like a reasonable person of her age, Victoria sets out to walk. Now it used to be there was a purpose in walking up Fillmore. I mean there was a time it was just alive with folks. It used to remind me of the marketplace in my village. I mean there was music coming out of the shops and anything you wanted to get, it could be found on Fillmore Street. Seemed like the street was the promise of everything that could be here for colored folks. It was a magic place. Folks used to call it the Harlem of the West. But they tore down that Fillmore and left it like it is now, it's nothing but shadows and memories, and empty lots where there used to be children being born and futures being made. Well, Victoria, she's still got something stuck in her side so she starts to picking up her pace. She's clutching that small handbag she had decided to carry that morning and almost running down the block. In her haste she missed a curb and tripped. She was caught at the elbow by a business suited gentleman who seemed to be going somewhere important. He broke her fall and lifted her back onto the sidewalk.

"Watch your step, ma'am."

Victoria pulled away in shock as if she had been attacked, and rushed down the street, causing a driver to slam on his car's brakes to avoid hitting the frightened woman. The gentleman stood on the corner bewildered. I told Victoria that she had better get back inside quickly if she didn't want to be seen, but she wouldn't hear it. "He only saw me because you have me rushing so." Then she said something else I couldn't quite catch, she kind of spoke into her neck, letting her collar swallow the words. I had to tell her to stop mumbling so I could understand her. Well, Victoria was so hot she raised her voice and was almost yelling, "You're always bothering me! They do not see me except when you are talking and making me lose track of where I am going. It is your fault I tripped. You're always trying to make trouble. Sometimes I wish you'd just go away." Well, I'm not answering that, I know she's picking at me now, but I don't have a word to say. I just move off a bit and we walk in silence.

After a few blocks Victoria started up again, "Well, of course I do not mean for you to go away forever, but just be still more often. On evening walks I enjoy your company, but sometimes I just wish you'd hold your peace. My grandmother sent you to help me, not to make me trip and lose my place."

Now her grandmother did not send me anywhere. I know that, and she knows that too. But she has this way of forgetting whatever it is that she doesn't see the sense in remembering and remembering all the smallest most foolish details. Like she could tell you the color roses that were in the bouquet on her grandmother's grave fifty years ago, but she couldn't tell you what her next-door neighbors look like.

"But it was your fault. You know how poorly I slept last night, but here you are berating me. I see what I have to see, and say what I have to say. That does not make me foolish. Seeing doesn't make my life less peaceful, and it doesn't make more people see me, no matter what you might say."

Victoria drew back and stopped up short in the middle of the next block. She raised her voice again when I pointed out that she had to admit that someone always sees a Negro. "That's the most ridiculous thing I've heard you say in weeks, and you have been quite absurd in your conversation. Well, for one thing, I am not a Negro."

By this time she was winded. She decided to rest, as she often did, on the small wooden bench in the mini-park on the corner where her school friend Darlene's house once stood. She reached the bench and slowly sat down, feeling the weight of the years her spirit usually denied. People moved past her and around her, but they did not seem to see her. No one spoke to her, no one even looked at her. Victoria smiled; I could tell she was comfortable in her solitude.

"It's not true," this time she had quieted her voice. She had her school marm voice on and I knew I was due for one of her lectures. "You are nothing but trouble. That's just what Darlene used to say, just like you, 'Why don't you like being a Negro?' And you are just like her, confused. Go ahead, hide behind that scrawny tree, it won't change the fact that you have no comprehension. You've been coming to visit me for years and you still don't understand."

Now, I wasn't hiding behind the tree, I was leaning up on it because I was trying to put some space between me and Victoria. Victoria got up, smoothed her skirt, and then moved to the far end of the bench, where she sat back down. An elderly man, hoping to gather some coins to buy an evening brew to ease the gnawing that lived inside his gut, saw her talking to me, snapping at the air and waving her neatly gloved hands. She did not see him hovering under the light as she continued her conversation.

"I am the clear one. You are the one who is confused. How could I like or dislike being something that I am not?" She paused but I refused to respond. "What a ridiculous thing to say. Of course, I was colored once. But not anymore. Now I'm mostly light.

"The night my grandmother died, angels came to me in a dream. They were white with pink cheeks, as all angels are, with curled golden hair. They played on harps that had sunbeams where there were supposed to be strings. If you looked at those sunbeams as they vibrated when the notes were played, you could see a glistening white soft and cool moving in time to the gentle notes. When I found out my grandmother had died during the night, I knew that what I had seen was the angels singing my grandmother into heaven. The family all talked about me when I wouldn't cry at the funeral. Why should I have? My grandmother was inside of the light. They talked about me because I even refused to wear black, choosing instead my white Sunday dress and a pair of long white stockings. I was getting closer to the light, and I have not stopped getting closer since. Every day, every week, just a little brighter, just a little nearer," Victoria proclaimed.

With that Victoria stood up, smoothed her skirt again, and started walking back up the street. The gray haired man yelled at her through his cracked lips, "Hey, Colored White Gal, you are as crazy as the day is long, and for your information you are still as b-l-a-c-k as me. That spells black in case you ain't with it. Tinted. Colored. Light. Crazy as a two-legged centipede. Damn fool woman." He dug into his pocket and counted the change he found there. "Thirty-seven cents short. Best get cracking," he mumbled as he moved down the street, stopping the nearest pedestrian and asking for a bit of help.

Victoria trembled as I reminded her that I had already cautioned her about the loudness in her voice. "But it is your fault he saw me. Stop fussing at me and I will not need to raise my voice." She reached Sutter Street and turned the corner, picking up her pace so that she became a streak moving down the block. No one bumped into Victoria. No one even seemed to see her.

Victoria was tired, and walking much more slowly, when we got to the house. Still she made sure to keep just a couple of steps in front of me to let me know I didn't have to bother trying to say one word into her ear. Now, I have been telling this lady she's a bit tetched since I first met her. Even if she didn't agree, you'd think by now that it'd be water swallowed in the sand for as many times as she hears it. I didn't have much to say to her anyhow. You know a body gets tired of being blamed for something she not only didn't do but didn't even think about doing.

Dawa, the woman that lives on the top floor of Victoria's building, was leaning up against her husband Ruben as we were walking up. Victoria thinks it is quite improper for people to sit on front steps. "That's what they have parlors for," she used to say, when the two were just courting. For the longest time Ruben would walk on by, winking and blinking and flashing his dark eyes, and Dawa would be sitting at the top of the stairs, just people-watching and enjoying the sun. He always had a ready question and she always had a quick answer. After a few months of dancing around each other, Dawa let Ruben go on and move in. And, a few years after that, they went and got married. Of course Victoria thought they had gotten married much earlier, and who was I to tell her different.

When we walked up to the front step I see Ruben lean over and kiss Dawa real soft on the cheek. Now, when you look at Ruben you see Cree Indian mixed up with the African, shining all through him, hair a little loose, long almond eyes like some ancient piece of jet, and high cheekbones. I see he's holding her hand, but then he drops it and throws both of his hands up in the air and shakes his head in disgust. He is gesturing to Dawa's brother Ranger, who is standing with his head hanging, looking kind of sheep-dogged.

I remember when that Ranger was the dandy of Fillmore Street. Always neat, turning on his heels and singing some line to a young girl. Always had an easy line and a quick smile. A popular fellow, Dawa's brother. Where she's all spice and hot sauce, he was smooth chocolate syrup. I mean before, of course. Well, we are too far away to hear, but I can see that Ruben is saying no kinda way to something and dressing Ranger up and down one side then the other. Whatever he is saying, I can see "no" wrapped around it all kind of ways, in his stance, and his eyes driving dark into Ranger, and in the fire glow around him. He is full of n-o.

Dawa is all pregnant and has a caftan falling loose around her. She looks like some kind of a round watermelon all green and full with those locks pulled back into a pony tail. Dawa's face is all full and round, takes after her mother Lucille, and the woman's mouth is about always open and flapping. Well, right then, she was rubbing her belly trying to get some kind of comfort from the baby, or give it, I suppose, but either way it isn't working. Ruben seems fed up, he walks up real close to Ranger and says something straight on, one of those don't-take-another-step kind of things, and Ranger he just stands there openhanded. Then Ruben opens the door, turns back, and gives a hard look and last comment to Dawa before he closes the door just a little too firmly.

Dawa, her hand at her ear, is waving his last comment away. It always tickles me how those two squabble. Victoria thinks its tawdry, unladylike, and lewd. When Dawa has a problem with you, she will let you know it and she will get loud. I have stayed amazed that Victoria continues to acknowledge her whenever she is seen. Secretly, though, I think it's because she knows that if she didn't at least nod her head to Dawa, Dawa would start yelling out Victoria's name, and bring a crowd around until everyone could see Victoria. Victoria denies this, but then she denies everything I tell her. The woman can certainly see that light she is always talking about, but she does not have a clue how to use all the information it brings. Humph.

Well, Victoria takes that moment to slip past all three of them on the little path that leads to her basement apartment. The evening is kind of balmy for San Francisco. Ranger sits down next to Dawa, and I squeeze next to him in the space that is left. He kind of shivers when I sit down, tickles me. Now, Ranger is his father's boy, for sure. Must be about six foot two and thin as a rail; well, some of that comes from the genes, but most of it comes from that dope he likes to smoke. One thing though lately he got that smile back. Ranger got this crooked smile where one side of his mouth tip up higher than the other and shows all his big straight teeth. He flash that smile and folks around him start to grinning too. For a few years his eyes was all flat and gray, and his mouth was always dry and set in a thin line. Now, though, he got that grin back almost as wide as before. Ranger lives on the streets, off the streets, and through the streets. He's all the time receiving information, and shivering it off. Wasn't always that way, but now he's left a piece of himself in some of those dark alleyways, and he keep going back to look for it. I keep thinking he's gonna wise up and realize that it's gone forever. I mean he ought to take what's left of his insides, including that quivering bellyful of experience that left all kind of scars all over his insides, and be happy he's alive. But you can see he's not so sure he wants to do that.

I hear Dawa pushing aside whatever was just said, "Sketch came running by this morning on his way to the beach."

They favor a bit, Ranger and his son, but Sketch, he takes more after Dawa with those round eyes, and then she's got those long locks all down her back. They so long they've gotten bleached all red at the tips.

Dawa's leaned her head up against her brother's; he had his hand on her big old swollen belly. I don't think she's more than two three weeks away. It's a boy baby. Victoria got the nerve to be calling it a girl. That woman has never been able to call children. Sometimes she's right, but that's just a matter of odds. I mean with only two choices you bound to be right some of the time. But most times it's just a case of what she thinks the person should be having. Now she thinks that Dawa having a girl will calm her down. She thinks the gentle of a girl baby will settle the woman. That child have a girl, it'd be a wild cat. But that's of no matter because she's having a boy.

"Ranger, Sketch was so excited. He said you showed him

two bus tickets you bought to take him to D.C. to see the Vietnam memorial. He said you said it was the next part of you coming all the way back. Are you, Ranger? Because I'm about tired of watching you die. We're all pulling for you, and Mama's praying over you..."

Ranger put his fingers over her lips. "And Elise is cursing over me, and Jeannine is making those dolls like you showed her, and sticking pins in..."

"Yeah, well I doubt it, but you know you deserve it."

Ranger smiled at his sister. "Cheryl."

He rarely called her by her old name, and that got me interested. Now, I know it's time for me to go inside and make sure Victoria is alright. But I know Victoria is fine, and I don't really want to be pointedly ignored. So I just keep on sitting, watching the fog move closer to the hill.

"Sis, you know Ruben's wrong. Dope isn't on my mind all the time. It isn't even there most of the time anymore. I mean I've got it contained, but any moment it might just take its hooves and break out that corral. I know why Ruben doesn't want me around unless I'm all the way clean. And for some of us, that's what you got to do. But Dawa, I just don't happen to believe I'm one of them. I forgot almost everything. Almost everything, Dawa. It was like I had so many memories sucked up inside of me, and then being with Jeannine and Jamal. Being with them it made me look at all of it again, and again measure stuff, so I started forgetting, Dawa. I started controlling what I agreed to remember. But I remember family. I'm not ever going to be tearing it down, Dawa. You know you've always been safe with me—you, and your baby, and Ruben, and everybody. Dawa, I swear I know I'm lost, but I'm not all the way crazy. I'm fighting it, Dawa. That's the best I can do right now, Sis..."

"Lost? Well, why don't you put your eye on all the torches this family you haven't forgotten are carrying and walk that way? Maybe you'll find something there."

"Dawa, you need some things. You know they are gone

forever, but you still need them. I mean you need them to be a part of you, so you keep on going, but they're gone. And when that happens there's nothing you can finish, nothing you can really start. It's work just making each day pass through you, and holding on so you can make it to the next day. Dawa, sometimes just for a moment, don't you want to know that you got everything under control? Don't you want to know that it's all okay, right at that moment, even if it's just for a minute, because then it's another minute and then another minute and then just one more... I know I'm better because I used to try and get that feeling when I was hitting the pipe all the time. When I'm high I know all the answers. It's all so clear. It's just me and her, and she's telling me how sweet the world will be, and I'm listening and doing whatever I can just to keep her talking to me, another puff, and then another one. But now, Cheryl, now, sometimes I don't look for it. I hear her calling, but I just don't answer. I let it pass, even though I need it so bad, sometimes it's like I just..."

That man just hung his head and shook it. Pitiful, that's what I thought. Pitiful. And judging by the look on Dawa's face she wasn't too happy with none of that either. I'd say she didn't want to hear a bit of it. I was leaning closer into Ranger, and he was shivering and trying not to show Dawa. But she caught the last little roll of chill off of his shoulders, "Ranger, are you cold? The fog's not in yet. I don't think it's getting over the hill tonight."

"Dawa, seems like something is just breathing on my back. You know, like that feeling I told you I get sometimes when ghost lady is doing her little flash around the corner."

I'm just holding my mouth shut so the laughter won't fall out, because I think if I tried real hard I might be able to get him to hear something today. I've been working on him for a while, but that smoke kept him real distant. Far as can be. But now isn't the time to, uh, spook him.

"Ranger, what are you afraid of... I mean what exactly haven't you seen and survived? Because I just don't get it at all. You came back from the war with all your pieces, not like your friend Hoodoo. You came back with all your mind. You came back with a place to stay, and not long after that you had a real loving wife, a son, a job. Ranger, you gave all of it up. And for what? Ranger..."

Dawa sighed.

"You know, they've got this fungus in Vietnam that gets right between your toes. It can take years to get rid of it forever. Oh, you can get down to just a spot or two. Sometimes it even pretends it's all the way gone. But it's there. You can't see it, but it's there waiting to start growing again. I had a partner had jungle rot for fifteen years." Ranger let out a dispirited laugh, "Who knows, if he'd lived a few years longer, he might of had it for twenty."

Then Ranger stood up so quickly that I fell back into the railing on the step. He walked out to the curb and looked each way as if he was expecting someone. Then he came back and stood by Dawa.

"You know sometimes we walked for miles through their jungles. You looked around you and there were thousands of kinds of green. And you had to get good at looking and seeing the snakes and the dragonflies, and the young and old bamboo, and then the glint of steel. But sometimes I'd be walking and realize how beautiful it was in that place. I mean birds with different coos, and the hush of the leaves breaking, and I remember thinking, *if it was another time and we were different people, this would be something, something else...*"

"Ranger, put it to sleep. Whatever it was, that was then. You've been around ten times as many years as you spent over there. Let it rest, stop using it as an excuse for not moving on."

"Now you know when you put something to sleep, it always wakes up again. That'll wake up too, because it's now. The war is here now, Sis. Every sick, ugly, depraved thing one of us did over there, well, we're doing it here too, and now our children are carrying the same weapons over here that I shot over there."

"That's not the world, Ranger."

"It's my world. It's the one I live in, and the one you live next to. Dawa, you know what I'm afraid of? I'm afraid of not living long enough to get back into the world you keep telling me exists. I'm afraid that even if I do get back, I'll get hit by a bullet ricocheting off of that old world I just left. When I was over there we kept talking about coming home, getting back to *the world.* Sometimes, there is no getting back. Oh, some of you gets back, but some of you just can't make the trip."

Dawa opened her mouth and then changed her mind about what she was going to say. Instead she reached up from the step and grabbed Ranger's hand. She placed it on her womb. "Feel that?" I saw her belly rumble as the baby shifted around. "What you think I'm having?"

"Boy."

Dawa answered him sarcastically, "Because that's *best*?"

"No, because it is. You know I called all three of Jeannine's."

"No, you didn't. You called boy three times."

"And I was right two out of three times."

The two of them laughed, and Ranger eased back down between me and his sister. Dawa looked hard into his eyes and wouldn't blink, and after a while I could see what she was seeing. Neither one of them was speaking, they were just looking at each other. Dawa, it was like she was pressing back this film that was coating his eyeballs until she could see the two of them years before. There was Dawa and her big brother running down the park hill that was covered by fog, open-mouthed, eating the mist as if it was a magic syrup. And then there they were with her watching him swing across the monkey bars, skipping three rings at a time, suspended in the air for just a moment between each sweep, fly, grasp steel, fly, grasp steel, fly... And then there they were at the dinner table with both parents, two other brothers, and Elise, the oldest girl. It was the day Ranger left home. "Don't lie to me, boy! You smoking that reefer?" His father was yelling. "Not and stay in this house! Not my house! You think I don't know about you sneaking into clubs and hanging in the alleyways! Boy, I was helping hang 'grand opening' signs at some of the places you frequent. I've known too many people in this area for too long for you to be giving me your lies! You might get your mother to go for those sugar-coated lies, but not me! I tell you, Lucy, we need to send him home to my father. Let him work some land for a while and get happy about what he has here. I tell you!"

"You're not sending me nowhere!" Ranger had shot back. "Talking about weed, like you so holy and pure with your sour-mash breath!" Before the young man had finished the sentence, he felt the back of his father's hand and the edge of a watch band across his cheek cutting a deep gash. Ranger jumped up. "Old man, you don't have to send me nowhere! I've got places to go!"

Suddenly Ranger turned his head to the street as a car whizzed by. He brought the film back across his eyes, letting out no more of their history. Dawa's eyes filled with water as she looked at her brother. She reached her hand up to her brother's face and pulled her fingers across the narrow ridge that ran from the corner of his left eye to the middle of his cheek. Ranger flinched as if it still hurt to be touched there.

"Hell of an eviction notice," she murmured.

Ranger smiled. "Yeah, Dad could of made his point without all the fireworks. Seemed like the only thing he saw when he looked at me was what I wasn't doing, and who I couldn't measure up to, and how I didn't have no future." They both shook their heads together and pulled on their chins like Elliott Senior used to do; then Dawa made her voice as deep as she could and rolled it out like a path of gravel.

"Lucy, boy gone crazy."

And Ranger joined in, "That Cheryl Linn too. She has too much mouth for any little girl."

And then the both of them together, "I'm not sure we wouldn't been just as well off in Texas. Maybe better." The two of them laughed softly at the memory. Then Dawa let out a long breath, "Ranger..."

"Sometimes, Dawa, I feel like I'm stuck in a game of musical chairs. You know, running around and trying to get one of the last chairs. But there's never an empty chair for me. So I keep getting kicked out of the game. No matter how fast I run, I never get there quite in time. Stay off Ruben, Sis. I know Ruben will help me with Sketch. No matter what he thinks of me, I know he'll help me with the boy. And that's what matters. I can't keep me together and always look after him, too. And Sketch is starting to get used to Mike,"

"Mitch."

"Whatever."

"No, Elliott, not whatever, Mitch. Jeannine's husband's name is Mitch. And since they've had a couple of children together it seems like you could twist your mouth around to say it with some respect. Anyway I thought you knew him in Nam."

"I met him. He got on my ass about spending too much time walking around by myself. I didn't like him then and I don't like him now. Spit-and-polish army. From soldier to pig."

"Probation officer."

"That's what I said."

Dawa smiled, "Well, he gave notice. I think after all that mess with Jamal, he had enough. Jeannine says he's training to drive a bus."

"That man loves a uniform, don't he?"

"He takes good care of Jeannine and Sketch too."

"Sketch don't like him."

"You don't like him, and Sketch loves you. Anyway,

Sketch isn't used to living with a drill sergeant. The man can be kinda heavy-handed."

"Dawa, what I'm saying is I know Sketch is going to be alright because he's got enough of you to hold onto."

"He's got you. I mean you are back, aren't you?"

"I'm getting close, Sis. Sometimes I get up, and the morning is so fresh, so clean, I can just feel it swirling all around me. I know that I'll make it through the day—and other days, other days I forget why, Dawa. I don't know what I'm coming back to, or coming back for."

Then Ranger sits down, jumps back up, and walks back to the curb. I swear between that man's red eyes and baggy pants and bright green shirt that man could be a jack-in-the-box clown, up, down, up, down. And Dawa is frowned up and watching him too.

"Ranger, you expecting company?"

"No, Dawa, you know it's just hard for me to sit still, that's all, and I know how you love to sit out on anybody's stoop, but nowadays I've just gotten more comfortable being indoors."

"Come on up. To hell with Ruben. It's my house too."

"Naw, that's alright. I don't feel like being between you two and your fireworks. I just came to check in."

"Ranger, why can't you just stop? I mean you could do whatever you wanted to, always. You taught me to go that way. Why can't you just stay clean?"

"I'm doing better, I swear I'm doing better, Dawa."

I got right close until I was almost breathing into Ranger's mouth. His eyes were lined with red, and the pupils were flat and open a little too wide. The black was almost filling the bulbous socket. It looked like it had been a day or two since he'd been covered by sleep. He leaned right through me and gave Dawa a kiss on each cheek.

"Ranger, you don't look good. You're not messing up, are you? Tell me Ruben's just tripping."

"Cheryl, through all of this have I ever lied to you?"

"Ranger, you lie all the damn time. You lie about what you need some money for, you lie about the job you don't have and haven't looked for, you lie about the last time you spent some real time with Jamal, you lie about the last time you made Mama cry...don't get me started. Have you ever lied?"

"But when you ask me to tell you true where I am, or where I'm going to be, so you can reach me..."

"Ranger, you are nowhere, and you keep spinning in one spot. At this point, what is there to lie about anymore?"

"I told you I was coming back from the edge, and I did. I told you two years ago that Jamal would know me as more than a friend, and he does. I told you I'd never kill anyone for drugs, and I haven't. But am I messing up? Dawa, I'm doing better than I was, and not as good as I guess I should be..."

Just then Victoria opens the door, dressed in a heavy coat like she's going out for the evening, and she tips her head to me like she wants some company. Well, to tell you the truth, I'm comfortable right where I am. Why would I want to go traipsing around with her and her bad attitude? In fact, why would she want to go anywhere? Seems like she's been seen enough for today. But I guess she had something to prove to someone. Sure wasn't me. I know folks can see her. And before I get a chance to point out the obvious, well, Ranger and Dawa they both notice the door cracked open and Ranger calls out, "Hey, ghost lady, you never did thank me for that white rose I left on your doorstep. That's alright. I know you liked it."

Victoria turned to him and for a minute I thought she was going to speak, but then she thought better and scooted right back inside. "That woman never speaks." Ranger muttered under his breath..

Dawa laughed, "She doesn't like to be seen."

Ranger snorted, "Who does? Besides you, of course. You one loud-assed woman that loves to be seen." Ranger rubbed his hand across Dawa's middle, and felt her baby kick again. "Call him Mandela or something. You know, a free name."

"I call him or her whatever I please, thank you. And you can bet it's gonna be a look-at-me name. Nice and loud."

"Dawa, I wanted to hit that pipe real bad the last two days. I want to smoke real bad every day. But I spent the last two days just walking, not smoking, or hustling, or slinging, just walking. Oh, I've been wanting something real bad. I can smell it coming out of people's windows, and it smells so ugly, and so sweet. But I've just kept moving, just kept moving. Like I did when I was a kid. But you know, wherever I walked, I didn't see anything but people already dead, on their way to dying, or ought to be dead. Did you hear about that old Chinese man they found slumped over his steering wheel? Just a couple of blocks from here? I saw him die. Must have been his heart, he was just putting the key in the ignition when he grabbed at his chest. I could see his mouth moving, and I think he saw me out of the corner of his eye. But I didn't move towards him. I just watched as he flailed for a couple of minutes and then slumped over."

"You didn't try and call 911 or nothing?"

"It was his time to go."

"Hope you feel that way when it's your time."

"One thing we know for sure, I'll be ready."

"Since you don't seem to be ready to live, what makes you so sure you're ready to die?"

"For one thing, because I've been inside of death, and next to death, and around death, and the cause of it, so many times. I'll be ready for it. See, Dawa, you see a difference between life and death. You think the two are different. I know they ain't. Dying is what you spend your whole life doing after you're born. Just like a piece of fruit. It grows, it ripens, and then the rest of its time, it's getting eaten up, by mold, by people. It doesn't matter. It's dying.

"People like to pretend they're constantly growing, but hey, after nineteen, twenty, your body gets weaker, you start getting lines, some gray here and there. Hey, you're dying. Most people just don't want to admit it. I'm not so different, just more honest about it, that's all.

"Anyway, after the old man slipped on out, I walked up past the vacant blocks. The ones they keep saying they're going to put some houses on. Those blocks were full of houses and stores and everything else when we were kids. Now, they're just torn up lots, been redeveloped from a neighborhood into a little doorway to hell.

"But you know how some of mama's friends have taken to planting in one of them? I think they are trying to reclaim it or something. Well, I was walking past that corner, and it was high with some collard green plants, and some scrawny excuses for corn, and there was Hoodoo crouched in a corner leaning on the fence. He had his fake leg taken off, and it was standing up next to him like some kind of a sentry. He was wearing some recycled army fatigues, and had on one of Daddy's old sweaters that mama had given him a few months ago when he went to visit.

"Now, you know Hoodoo, he tries to stay clean. Even when he gets out there, he makes an effort, but then he was just covered in dirt. His nails were caked with it, and there was dried blood on the front of the sweater. He had a cigarette in his hand, but it was about to burn his fingers. Hoodoo's into scag now, you know. Says he hurts all the time. Even the leg he doesn't have still hurts him. You know they never did fix him up right. Well, he was off in a nod, and smelled like he had messed in his pants. I couldn't just leave him like that. So I tried to get him to come with me and get cleaned up. I figured Mama would let us crash at her place. He just cursed me out and told me to get my skinny chicken behind out of his face.

"Now, you know Hoodoo's saved my life too many times for me to leave him like that, so I tried to pull him on his feet, and damned if he didn't haul off and take a swing at me. Of course he missed. I decided to leave him be for a minute, and go to the store nearby and get a little vodka to take the edge off the evening. Then I'd come back and sit with Hoodoo, make sure nobody messed with him, you know. When he woke up a little, I'd help him, you know, pull it a little more together.

"I go down the block to the store, and just as I get outside the door, who do I see coming up the street, looking for me, but Jamal. And that boy was just smiling, showing his relief that I wasn't all cracked out. But when I told him to go on home, and that I wouldn't be coming with him, I mean straight away coming with him, well, the first alive face I'd seen in hours, started shining full of scorn for me. I didn't know how to explain how much I didn't want him to come with me and see Hoodoo like that. He knows Hoodoo has a problem, but he didn't need to see the man all tore down, not like that. So I made up some kind of half-baked story about where I was going, and how he couldn't come. But he wants to, and gets mad because he sees that I really won't let him come. Then he notices the bag in my hand, and starts talking about how he can see that I'm getting ready to mess up royal. He just turned his back to me, and walked away real disgusted like. And, Dawa, I couldn't blame him, but I sure couldn't take him with me. I mean I couldn't blame him for not believing that I wasn't messing up, but I still didn't want to see that venom he had for me in his eyes. But hey, what could I do?

"I spent the night with Hoodoo and got him in a hospital the next morning. They say they're going to have to cut him open because something is blocking his intestine again. I swear they're still digging out pieces of shrapnel from that man's belly. I'm alright, Sis, doing better. In fact, I got to go by Mama's and show Sketch that I'm alright. I think I'll see if Mama is frying some chicken tonight."

"Well, it's Friday, isn't it?" Dawa took Ranger's hand and squeezed it. "You want me to visit Hoodoo for you?"

"That's alright. They're moving him over to Oakland

tomorrow, and he'll probably be in some kind of a shelter the day after that. Shovel them in, shovel them out. You just make sure you help Jeannine keep up with Sketch."

"You come by tomorrow and check in on me, okay, Ranger? You know the baby could come early."

"If it's as impatient as you are, I guess it will. But hey, more likely than not I'll see you tomorrow evening. I'm cool, Sis. Really. Last couple of days been rough, but I'm cool. Really..."

Then he looked up and down the street one last time before he started walking around the corner towards Fillmore Street. He threw out his left leg and then pulled in his right, trying to put a little snap in his walk, trying to look like the Ranger he used to be, but then when he took another step, seemed like he tripped over nothing and had to catch himself. That stumble wasn't lost on Dawa. She called out his name, and he heard her too, but he didn't turn around, just kept on walking with his one-sided jaunt.

Dawa sat there for a few minutes and I sat next to her. I wanted to tell her not to worry, but she was right to worry. We just sat there quiet next to each other, and then she got up and slowly climbed those stairs, each footstep falling heavier than the last one. Well, I didn't feel like sitting out on the step by myself so I went on inside to tell Victoria she could come back out, though I was hoping she was in for the night. I can tell that this is a night for me to stay close to Victoria, and I really don't have a mind to be bothered with that old biddy right now. That Victoria is always putting a wrinkle in my day.

4. Friday Dinner

Ranger had to ring the bell to get into his mother's house. She had taken his keys away a couple of years before, and even though he came by regularly, he never asked her to return them, and she never offered. Sketch answered the door, saw his father, grunted and went back upstairs to his room. Ranger yelled up after him, "Hey, boy, I don't even get a hello?"

Sketch turned around and looked at him, and then without a word turned back and went upstairs. Ranger smelled potatoes boiling and heard chicken sizzling in the kitchen. His mother's voice called out,

"Elliott, is that you? I thought you said you were done worrying me."

Ranger walked into the kitchen and put his arms around his mother's waist. "Hey, African Queen Mother, my apologies. But I told you to *stop worrying*. What's up with Jamal? I don't think all that attitude is offa me."

"I don't know. He came in like a thunderbolt, went upstairs, and started to blasting his music. I had to fight for him to turn it down. You know he doesn't tell me what's wrong like he used to. Maybe he was just worrying about you." Lucille paused and looked up at her son. "I know I have been. I had Sketch to go over to that hotel you stay in and leave a note for you to call. That was two days ago. Junior..."

Lucille was just over five foot tall and only slightly rounded at the hips. Next to her son she seemed even shorter. She leaned back and looked at his face and saw that his eyes were too watery and his hands trembled slightly.

"When you last eat, boy?" she asked, happy that her voice had not cracked.

"This morning. I'm fine, Mama. Whatever you think you see, you're wrong. I'm fine. You need some help?"

"I need the table set. I called Jamal and asked him to see to it, but he ignored me."

"I'll go get him." Ranger leaned over and gave his mother another kiss on the cheek. "You know I love you, Mama. You always took good care of me, and now you take good care of Jamal too. Thank you, Mama."

Lucille turned back to her pan, forking a juicy chicken breast and laying it on the paper towels. She shook her head and smiled, "Are you going to get Jamal or stand here talking all evening? I felt you were coming. I told Jamal, too, but he just pooh-poohed me. And yes, you don't have to ask, I have plenty of gravy for the potatoes I'm getting ready to mash."

"Mmmmm," Ranger laughed, "I did something right today. Must have..." and he left the kitchen and went up the stairs to find Jamal.

When Ranger was clean he came by his mother's house for daily visits with his son and mother. Sometimes Lucille let Ranger live with Jamal and her, after he was released from jail, and after he promised that this time he was going to make it, that this time he'd stay clean, stay straight, do right by her and Jamal. And whenever he said it he meant it. He meant he would try. He meant he wanted to, at those moments, more than anything he wanted to do right.

Those were the times when the house hummed again. Lucille loved to watch Jamal and Ranger sitting together on the sofa, second-guessing a football game, "He's going to run it in, no he's not, he's going to pass it to..." And she loved the way they talked on rainy evenings, the way Ranger would tell Jamal the stories no one else in the family was allowed to hear. The tears he brought back from Vietnam, the wounds that no doctor could see, the wounds that still bled, that had turned part of his spirit to gangrene. But inevitably the draw was too great, and Ranger stumbled. First a small slip, a dip in the pool followed by remorse and guilt, and then a longer swim, until he was, at last, submerged again. Ranger always held onto one part of himself. He would leave before Lucille was forced to put him out. And Lucille and Jamal would once again be alone in the flat, comforting each other, and denying their own pain.

Jamal was a so-so student. School bored him. His mother had taught him how to read, and his father had give him a handle on division and multiplication; after that he didn't see the point. He didn't care about George Washington. He didn't like painting turkeys and pilgrims on Thanksgiving. He wanted to do more in science than plant seeds and make life-cycle charts. So instead of paying attention in class, he sat in the back of the classroom and drew. He started with cartoon figures, but soon started doodling the backs of heads of his classmates and the glasses falling over Mrs. Fleming's nose. When he fell in love, which he did frequently, he drew pictures of roses and left them unsigned in the girl's book or backpack.

Everyone knew Jamal, the artist. Despite three stints in juvenile hall for being caught creating his graffiti works on both public and private property, he continued to paint, can in one hand, pens in pocket. He'd cover walls, doors, billboards, anywhere that there was a space that he decided needed colors or had room for a statement that he knew needed to be heard. Lucille never understood why the boy wouldn't stick to painting in the sketchbooks she had bought him. He was so talented. She was sure he could become one of those people that drew advertising pictures or designed greeting cards or something. Maybe even a museum artist.

In Lucille's living room hung two colored-pencil drawings Sketch had finished. Whenever someone new came to visit the house she would proudly point them out and tell the visitor that her grandson, the artist, had done them. One time Mr. Lawry, one of the deacons at Third Baptist, actually offered Sketch money to paint the backdrops for the Christmas play. Sketch tried, but the barn background looked too modern. Jamal started by painting all the angels black and putting them in different African patterned cloths. It ended up becoming quite a scene with some of the parishioners wanting the money back that had been contributed for the paint supplies. Sketch ended up cursing them out with some of the foulest language he could find. Naturally the church folks ended up using the background they had been using for years and grumbling about the whole incident, and Mr. Lawry never offered Sketch any more painting work.

But those two pictures that hung on Lucille's wall were wonderful. One picture showed Lucille ready to leave for church. She was sitting in Elliott Senior's chair. When he was alive, no one but him ever dared to sit in that chair. In the picture Lucille was sitting up on the edge of the chair, as if she was still not sure if she really belonged there. She had on a small, pale yellow hat, with a white silk hatband, and a large white rose sloping off of the brim. Only a few carefully pressed curls showed from underneath the hat. Her eyes were small and seemed like they were full of tears, but her mouth smiled softly, making her cheeks even fuller. That day she had dressed in her white suit with a yellow satin blouse that Elise had sent up for her birthday. It was a Mother's Day Sunday, and she was to be honored at the church. She held her handbag in her lap, and although the picture caught her looking out, she seemed to have been looking far past the artist to another time, another world.

It was that picture that made Lucille know her grandson might actually become a "real" artist. She had stopped bothering him about getting into a trade school, and instead would come home with pencils and drawing pads to encourage him to get any old job while he worked on his pictures. She would call Dawa and ask what kind of paints he should have, and the two of them had planned a future for the young man.

The other picture was a picture of Ranger. Ranger refused to pose for his son, so Jamal used a picture that Ranger had sent his mother when he was in the Nam. It showed his father in camouflage pants and a green tee-shirt, arm thrown around what was to become Jamal's godfather, Hoodoo, who was leaning over with a stick in his hand, drawing, Jamal had been told, signs of protection into the sand. It was after that picture was taken, Ranger had told his son, that Hoodoo had lost his leg. Hoodoo always said it was because the photograph drained the power out of his spell and painted it on the film. Ranger said, "Sooner or later luck always runs out." Jamal loved his father's face in that picture, the ways the eyes sparkled, and the way you could tell he was laughing full out, teeth showing and full lips quivering with the joke. Jamal had drawn only his father's head, with its short Afro and smooth-skinned sable face. He had even used the side of the picture to shade in the glow of sweat that made his father seem even younger.

Lucille had thought that if she encouraged Jamal to paint at home he would stop painting on other people's walls. Jamal had done three stints in jail for vandalism and Lucille never did see the point. "M'dear," Jamal would come close and kiss her on the cheek like he always saw his father do, "M'dear, it's not the same. When I do a tag or a piece, everybody knows I'm here. It's not just for the family, it's for everybody. I'm good, M'dear. Really good."

"Boy, I know you can draw. I just don't see why you mess up other people's property. I mean you can do a picture on our garage if you got to paint."

"M'dear, it's not the same. You go on a bus and see Sketch, I've been there. You go to the beach and see Sketch and Cookin are live, and people know Casey and me exist, we're something. We're not just some shadow so a white woman can clutch her bag and start hustling down the street because she sees us. We're not just some drug slinger Five-O can pull over to the side and throw up against the wall because he wants to. We're everywhere, we can even get in their dreams. And, M'dear, when you do it right, when you do it jammin uptight, no one paints over it, it just stays there for years until the rain and the salt and the sun bleach and wash it away, but by then thousands of people have seen it. Understand?"

"No. I understand this picture of your father, and I understand this picture of me. And I understand those paintings in that Sargent Johnson book your Aunt Cheryl Ann gave you. The ones that show Harriet Tubman running away to be free. But I don't for a minute understand how painting a name that's not even your name on a wall has anything to do with being somebody."

Jamal had lived with his grandmother since he was twelve, visiting his mother on weekends and spending most of summer vacations with her. He didn't want to move to Oakland with his mother and Mitch, his stepfather, and his half-sister and brother. Jamal didn't care for Mitch one way or the other. He thought he was too rigid, and he really didn't like taking orders from anyone who wasn't his real father, especially a man who talked so bad about his father, as if all Ranger was was a crack fiend and a thief.

Of course, Jeannine and Ranger had long been apart. Once Jeannine understood that he was a lover of the snow queen, she cut all the cords that bound Ranger and her, and never looked back. It was like she just took the love she had for him and packed it into one of those boxes she kept loaded with things she never looked at, in the basement of the house she and Mitch shared in Oakland.

The main reason that Jamal had wanted to stay with his grandmother was that his father lived there so often. Even when Ranger was using drugs, he came by to visit now and again. He wasn't a stranger. And when he came, he'd take Sketch on a walk or a bus ride and make him show him all of his new pieces. Ranger never told Sketch to stop painting on walls; he just told him to be the best at it.

Jeannine agreed to let Jamal stay at his grandmother's over Mitch's objections. She wanted her son happy, and she felt Lucille needed someone else close by. Jamal had already started doing badly in school, and she felt that he and Ranger might help each other through the rough years. The boy was getting to be more than she could handle, and he hadn't taken to Mitch like she thought he would.

Dinner was full of edges and steep hills. Ranger tried to get Jamal to talk, and got one-word answers in reply. Lucille would demand that Sketch show his father some manners. Jamal would mutter under his breath. They would all eat another bite of food. Sketch tried to leave the table early, but his father demanded that he sit back down. "Not that it's any of your damn business. But I was with Hoodoo last night. I told you I'm doing alright, Jamal. Hoodoo was sick."

"Hoodoo's always sick."

Lucille cut in, "Billy's no better, Elliott? I thought you said you both were in the program."

"No. Hoodoo couldn't hang, Mama. You know he hurts all the time, and he needs to take stuff just to keep his insides cooled down. He's in the hospital, but they said they expected to discharge him in a day or two. Jamal, now what's getting to you? I'm not required to check in. I'm the father, you are the child."

Sketch sneered at his father, "At least that's how it's supposed to go, right?"

Lucille cut her eyes at her grandson and sternly reprimanded him, "You are not showing your father any disrespect in my house. You hear me, young man?"

"Yeah," Sketch answered.

"Excuse me," Lucille seemed to grow an inch in her seat as her voice got firmer, but no louder.

"Yes, M'dear."

No one talked for some minutes. Ranger began to suck the marrow out of a chicken bone and Sketch followed suit. Lucille smiled, seeing them ignoring each other as the bones cracked and they sucked out the juices. Lucille started to clear the table. Sketch jumped up to help, trying to get away from his father, who followed him into the kitchen.

"Come on, boy," Ranger reached his arm out and caught his son's shoulder, "Talk to me. Some girl put you down? Some one mess up one of your tags? When I'm wrong, you can have all the attitude you want, but, son, I really wasn't messing up. Talk to me. "

"Pieces. I do pieces not tags. Tag is just a name. I do more."

"Jamal. I know this isn't all about not seeing me for a couple of days. I mean that's the way it's always been."

Sketch walked into the other room and picked up a sketchbook and started drawing a picture of Victoria. He drew her like he had seen her at the beach, with her felt hat pulled over her hair and her skirt scraping the top of her ankle. Ranger walked into the room and stood over his son watching him draw.

"She's skinnier than that. And no wrinkles in the face. When did you see the ghost lady?"

"See her all the time. She lives downstairs from Dawa. Always talking to herself."

"You know, you're getting good."

"Were you ever good at anything, Dad? I mean besides slinging dope."

"Actually, I'm a pretty sorry drug dealer, smoke up all the profits. I think I'd a been a good explorer. You know I should of been around with Matthew Henson or someone, so I could of gone exploring. I used to sing a taste in high school, too. I wasn't a half-bad carpenter. And you know, when I was in high school, I was sure I was headed for some major league baseball career."

"No, Dad, I mean really good at something. Something you didn't let go of... Real good."

"Just because you let go of something doesn't mean you weren't good at it. Hoodoo probably could of been a scientist or something. You know that man could do all kind of math problems in his head, I mean you could just run numbers and tell him to divide, and multiply, and do fractions, and he'd always be right on the money."

"Guess that served him well with his drug habit. A regular mathematical chemist."

Ranger ignored his son's comment, musing, "I never had a chance to find out just how good I was at anything. But I must of been talented, you didn't come out of nowhere. Must have been. I just didn't keep at it."

Sketch turned over a page in his book. "You going to let me draw you tonight?"

"Jamal?"

"Why you don't ever call me Sketch?"

"Because I named you Jamal. I don't make your grandmother call me Ranger. She named me Elliott."

"She doesn't understand. You're supposed to... You going to let me draw you?"

"I look kind of sorry. Need a shave and a bath."

"You gonna let me draw you?"

Ranger looked at his son, who would not let him get away. "I was good, real good at making a son. You fine, like your father used to be, smart, got a skill. Yeah, I was good at something."

Sketch smiled, "I asked you a question."

"Yeah, man, I'll get cleaned up and put back on this birthday shirt she gave me, and I'll sit for you. But you better not be taking all night. I mean, get the general idea, and then I'm done."

"You're not going out tonight, right? I mean we got all night."

"I'm planning on being here. But I'm not planning on sitting for you all night."

Ranger walked over and put his hand on his son's shoulder and leaned down. "You know you got your mother's smarts, and mine. Don't be a fool like me."

Sketch smiled, "Naw, Dad. I think one fool in the family is enough."

"Oh, we got more than one fool in this family. I'm just the worst. Let me go and get cleaned up for this portrait. This is the first, last, and only time I'm sitting for you. You got that, right?"

"Shit, when I get famous you're going to be begging me to draw you."

Ranger laughed as he walked up the stairs, and kept laughing as he closed the bathroom door and started to bathe.

5. Fillmo'e Street

she is a dark woman
treading water
in a life of hard choices.
wrong decisions
limited alternatives
stock-pens are embedded
in her eyes and mouth.

once she knew she was beautiful.

if you look closely
you can still feel
the edges of the fire that burned
in her eyes, on her skin
in the way her back arched
across fillmo'e street corners.

she wore her nails
sculpted in red
in those days
when that street
when this street
was ours

she sat on a barstool
snapped her fingers
and hunched her shoulders
as smoke rose between
the bandstand and counter
and the scene
got hot and sultry
and the music
pressed out the doors
and down the street.

further down
she slid in at jacks
had another cigarette lit,
flashed her teeth, laughed
as the club spun tight
shoulder to shoulder
thick smoke and blaring saxophone.

then she checked in with minnie,
bought a pitcher of beer and half-way
listened to some crazy poets
chant a continent of promises
with congo drum and shakeré
punctuating the rhythms
and a flute solo
bursting out over
the tastiest of love poems

maybe, maybe
she slipped into connie's
for some curried goat and coconut bread
or sweated spices next door
as leonard pulled another
sweet potato pie
out the oven and poured
his brown-red biting sauce
over smoking tender ribs
telling stories
as she savored another mouthful
then, when the street was ours.

she can see those days.
she knows them.
she remembers
before, before
imported cheese

before brandy-filled truffles
before double lattes
hand-made paper cards.

she sits on the iron-rimmed
privately owned bench
to rest her feet
and take the pinch
out of her back.
she holds the bitter in her mouth
sometimes spits it out at passers-by,
with steel in her stare,
there on that bench
on that corner
on that block
on that street
that was ours, that was hers
that was taken, that we let go
that is lost, that was fillmo'e
when the streets held the people
and the musicians had names
and the rhythm was blues,
and the downbeat was jazz
and the color
was black and fierce
like her.

It was late in the evening when Dawa and Ruben came outside. Dawa let Ruben hold onto her elbow as they came down the steep stairway, but when they reached the sidewalk, Dawa pulled away from Ruben. He laughed and pulled her close again. "I thought we were friends. Tell you what, for the rest of the night Ranger's going to live his life and we are going to live ours."

"And if they overlap?"

"When they do, we'll deal with it. Let's enjoy the evening. You know I'm in love with your big, hard-to-get-along-with pregnant self. Good thing too, because I'd be long gone."

"Stay or go, doesn't make a difference to me," Dawa retorted.

"You lie, you lie." Ruben leaned over her and gave her a kiss. They walked quietly and slowly down the street. Ruben was enjoying the edge of chill on the air, the feel of his arm around Dawa's waist, and two days laid out in front of him when he could actually take back a corner of his own life, pull it back from the sheaf of paper that flowed onto and off of his desk in relentless piles. They were pieces of paper which, with the right signature there, and the right number here, could change people's lives, assure them of one more semester in college. And even though there was some good in the purpose, the work itself was mostly rote. A line of criteria one side, a larger number of qualifying applications than the money could begin to fill. An impossible task of allocation. In a way Solomon had it easier, Ruben thought, whatever his decision had been, the child and women would keep on living. Some of the choices he made did not give that comfort.

He stopped and turned to Dawa. He leaned down and kissed her again. "You know I'm real glad we're doing this. I mean the baby, us."

"Well that's good, because it's a little late to change your mind."

"No. I know that lately I've been short with you a lot. But it's not you. It's the job and the city. I really, really..."

"...really *need* to get out of this city," Dawa cut in, finishing his sentence for him. Then she started walking again, moving slightly in front of Ruben. As they turned the corner onto Fillmore, she pointed towards the grocery store on the corner. "Remember, that's where you first met Ranger and me."

Ruben frowned, "I don't know if meet is the right word now, Dawa. You mean that was where I first encountered him, don't you? As I remember it, he was loud talking one of the finest-looking women I had seen in a long while, and demanding that she give him some pocket change, which she clearly could afford to do, seeing that she had plenty of money to buy whatever she was carrying in all those bags. So being the chivalrous gentleman I am, I came over and started to tell him to ease up on you."

"Without asking me if I needed your help, which I didn't," Dawa laughed out.

"Which is about what you said then, only I don't remember you smiling. But I do remember telling you I'd stand over to the side so that if you changed your mind or circumstances I'd be available."

"Yeah, and damned if Ranger didn't come all out of himself and start talking about he had a right to talk to me and you didn't."

"If I had had half a brain I'd a turned around right then and got away. I mean talk about a flashing sign saying "Problem in this family, no smooth sailing ahead." But no, I got caught looking at your nostrils flare up, and the little naps at the nape of your neck curl up, and you let out a cycle of epithets talking about everyone better just back off. Elliott needed to get the hell out of your face, and I needed to take my good Samaritan behind where it was needed, and everyone else on the street should mind their own goddamn business. You were just growling and showing your claws. And damn if your brother didn't just curse you over his left shoulder and walk on down the block."

"But not you. Suddenly you decide I need an escort home."

"No, suddenly I decided that I wanted to see if you kept that fire burning in all areas, and not just on street corners when you are loaded down with packages."

Dawa smiled to herself, "We were standing right here, when it was a club, and you convinced me to go inside with you and have a drink. They had a trio that day who were playing some real easy jazz. The piano was just trilling out like a brook of fresh water. I swear those notes just made me want to cool down and take a few deep breaths."

Ruben smiled and pulled his hand down her now full cheek slowly. "I always suspected it wasn't really my charming smile."

"Well, I'll give the smile credit for getting me to stop long enough to hear the music."

Ruben pulled on Dawa's hand gently, and they started walking again, down the hill. Both of them glad they had made the journey as far as they had. Ruben started in again, "But, baby, there's nowhere here to take you now, to hear the music like that. I mean not like it was on the blocks, nowhere to sit back, get close to someone pretty, make some space between the streets and your heart, just be yourself at home, but at the same time out. That's all gone."

"Ruben, there are all kind of places."

"Where we can be at home? Come on, Dawa, they've taken most of the street back. You can barely tell we ever had a hold to this place."

Dawa knew he was right. She remembered just after the family was settled in, her uncle took them on a walk down Fillmore. Her mother saw a dress shop where she would later apply for work, there was the used furniture store where

Elliott, Junior got his first job. In fact, Elliott's boss, Mr. Jones, was the one that gave Elliott the moniker of Ranger. The boy was always coming in a little late from work on the weekends. He would get up early and go, as he would tell Mr. Jones, exploring. He climbed through the steep hills of Sutro Forest, he scaled one side of Twin Peaks, he chased squirrels through the lonely woods in McClaren Park. He had loved the open ranges in Texas, and now he loved the patches of green that filled the borders of San Francisco. If there was an open space he claimed it, and in the claiming often lost track of the time and was late for his ten a.m. starting hour. So Mr. Jones, after hearing another one Elliott's why-I'm-late-today stories about this tree he climbed or that raccoon family he found, named him Ranger. The boy was never happy inside, could only work without complaining if he had had those hours to explore and be with himself.

In those years the street held all kinds of places to hear music. Dawa's parents went club hopping twice a month. It was a Friday night ritual: first they started with some smooth, hot jazz, and then they wound on down the street until they got some thick, smoking blues. Always running into friends and paying for a round of drinks, or being given one. There were restaurants, and flower shops, and the best shoestore in San Francisco, that's what Elise always said. There was the hardware store where her father worked for years. By the time she was ten, Dawa knew the names of every kind of hammer and screw and wrench. During the summers she sometimes went and visited her father at work for his lunch hour. Her father always had some new gadget to show her. A better way of making a wrench, a more up-to-date barbecue pit, a new kind of venetian blind. Yes, you could fix and furnish your house, buy a stereo and the records to play on it, and fill your refrigerator with food and your liquor cabinet with spirits without leaving the street. Then after going out and carousing on Saturday night, on Sunday you could go to that same street and find a place to pray. The street was the village marketplace in those days. Everywhere you looked, it seemed like almost every store you went into there were black people behind the counter, black people in front of the counter, and black people helping at the shelves.

Yes, indeed, the Everman family had arrived in the land of plenty. Just as much as Ranger loved to learn the hills and gullies in San Francisco, Dawa loved to live on this street. There was the variety store where she had bought her first lipstick, her first box of sanitary napkins, her first charm bracelet. There was the movie theater where she had first kissed Jamie. Well, she had first started to kiss him, really kiss him, and then Ranger came in and collared the boy and told him there wasn't no way that boy was going to be swapping spit with his sister. Jamie didn't say a word, just shrugged. Ranger figured his work was done and went over to sit with his own girlfriend, and Cheryl Linn had to wait until that afternoon when they walked through the park, to get a real kiss and start going steady with Jamie.

Dawa looked around the street as she walked, all of that was gone. Oh, there were still stores and restaurants. But most of the folks were white, and no one talked to each other when they walked down the street. People weren't calling "Yoohoo's" down the block, and telling this one to hold on up, or chiding that child for running ahead. It was still a successful street, full of businesses that kept their doorways clean, and overpriced displays in the windows, and curt salespeople behind the counters. But it sure didn't rock or swing like before. Dawa pulled up short in front of a large plate-glass window that sported a headless mannequin wearing a brightly colored full-length cotton dress. "Isn't this where Connie's restaurant used to be?" She turned to the clothes stores that now lined the corner.

Connie's was a Jamaican restaurant where she and Ruben had had their wedding party. Curried goat and curried chicken, fried plantain, and piles of coconut bread had been placed around the room on platters. There was even a rum-

and-orange-juice punch that made most folks not notice the missing champagne. What a party! They danced, and ate, and drank into the morning, and then Dawa and Ruben walked home to the place they had already shared for six years.

"It's all so different now, isn't it?" She leaned her head against Ruben. "But, Ruben, if we all leave, there won't be anything left. I mean if everyone gives up and leaves."

"Dawa, people aren't leaving. We're getting squeezed out."

"If we left, *we'd* be leaving. I want to take it back."

"Dawa, we're too busy fighting with each other to remake Fillmore Street, or any other place in this city. We could move to where there are more of us, more of a community. What you love is gone."

"What I love is you, and Mama, and Sketch, and Ranger, and all of you are here in San Francisco. And I kinda like the fog too, it took me a bunch of years. But I kind of like the fog, too."

"Dawa, we can visit the fog. Though I don't know why you would want to do that. And your mother can come and be with us, and Sketch's mom is already in Oakland, and Ranger, well, Ranger will be around no matter where we are..."

"I don't know, Ruben, I don't know. What about my school?"

"You know there are plenty of children in any city you go to. I mean there are even more over there, and more parents who can actually pay, Dawa..."

"But do they need it any more than the ones here?"

"No more and no less, Dawa."

Ruben had been trying to get Dawa to move out of the city since before she had become pregnant. In fact, it was her pregnancy that slowed down the process. Ruben had come up from Los Angeles and was used to being surrounded by blocks and blocks of his own folks. He was uncomfortable with being "other" so much of the time, with feeling out of sync. Oakland was more like home, more summer, more regular folks, and less hassle all around. He had only caught the tail end of the Fillmore Dawa so loved. By the time he came, they were already demolishing full blocks of Victorian houses. There was no Princess Theater. The famous Booker T. Hotel, where the Whispers had sung Dawa's parents into their twenty-fifth anniversary, was long gone. The block-long Long Bar that all the old folks told stories about was torn down. In fact, of all the landmarks Lucille talked about, it seemed like only the fish store and the Chicago Barbershop remained. He went to the barbershop with Dawa's father before he passed on. Ruben would go there and get the perfect trim on his Afro, which he kept just this side of long, a nice full crown around his high cheekbones and smooth chocolate face, and hear the men reminisce about a city he had never really seen. From the time Ruben had come to town, the street was in decline and he felt himself out of time with this place, and out of step with the neighborhood. He knew the spirit was being drained from other neighborhoods too, but at least in those cities there was a little more left, because, he reasoned, there was a little more to start with.

The baby started kicking Dawa's side. She stopped and stood still for a moment. Ruben saw her draw in her breath. "Let's go sit somewhere and have some tea or something, Dawa."

"No, let's go home. I'm tired anyway and have a mess of clothes to fold. Let's go on in."

She smiled up at him, "Wasn't for this street, we might not have met."

Ruben leaned down and kissed her on the lips and then next to her ear, "No, we would have met. I would have tracked you down until I found you."

"Oh, now I'm some game, huh?"

"Yup, and I'm the one who got caught."

The two of them laughed together and holding hands walked on home.

6. Making a Run

seems that pain
is the number of this year.
summer has been delayed
until after the revolution
while babies cry and cry.

everybody is hoarse
from screaming to deaf masters
and most find it hard to choose
between shins scarred
from kneeling, and death.

the prisons are so crowded
that they're putting more bars
on the streets, and iron and chains
on the doors, while the price of
cocaine is down, again
summer has been delayed
until after the revolution

Lucille stood in the doorway between the dining room and the living room, where her son and grandson were. Jamal sat across from his father on the sofa, large sketch pad resting on his knees, and box of charcoals open next to him. Ranger was in Elliott Senior's chair. Well, not in it so much as on it, barely touching its edge. He was perched on it, legs spread, elbows pressing into each thigh, chin resting on his clasped hands on the thickly flowered chair's front rim.

"Just like that," he was saying as he smiled and shook his head.

"I'm doing your head now. Keep that part still, Dad."

"Well, what were you doing the last fifteen minutes?"

"Two and a half minutes, and I was getting the outline of the chair so I could get you the right size."

"Damn, boy, the chair is always here. You're supposed to be drawing me."

"First, you won't pose for me, and now you're giving instructions. What's up with that?"

Jamal was laughing, happy to have his father with him. Happy to feel fresh air once again blow through the room.

Lucille watched them from the kitchen doorway, Elliott sitting in his father's chair, not deep into it like Elliott Senior had sat, but just on the edge, so he couldn't even appreciate the full stuffing of it. She saw that he wasn't enjoying the way its soft and firm, could wrap around a person and make them feel comfortable. Whenever Lucille was alone, she sat in that chair and conjured up the memory of her husband until she could almost feel him next to her, kissing the edge of her ear, as he told her to come closer because he had a secret to tell. That chair was a comfort, Lucille thought, watching her son balanced on its edge.

Lucille realized that they didn't even know she was in

the room, so she called out, "Elliott is just like his daddy, Jamal—always going to tell someone how to do something, and doesn't care if he knows how or not. Your grandfather always figured if he hadn't done it, he'd thought about it, so he had every right to an opinion."

Ranger sat up. "Let's take a break, boy."

"Nope," Jamal answered. "I just got started, and I'm not taking no kinda chances on you changing you're mind."

Lucille walked over to her son and kissed him on his head. "You just sit right there, Elliott. Why don't you lean back and take your ease, son?"

Jamal answered before his father had a chance to let a breath through his lips, "Because I already got him started in this position, M'dear, and no disrespect, but I got to keep going."

"I'm sorry, Jamal," Lucille smiled, "I certainly don't want to interrupt your work on my"—she stressed the my—"picture."

Ranger smiled at his mother's comment, and Jamal moved his charcoal up to catch the curve of the man's lips as he looked at his mother. Lucille was like that, claiming something right off, just to make sure that it was clear where it was going. Jamal knew he would tell her later that he was planning to hang it in his room. Maybe he'd compromise and put it in the hall outside his door. But no, this one was *his* picture. He already had given his grandmother one. But there wasn't any reason to worry about that just now.

Lucille touched Ranger lightly on the shoulder, "How you doing, boy, really? I see you're eating well, but how are you doing?"

Ranger sat up. Jamal sucked in his breath and cursed softly. His father saw the boy's frustration and returned to his pose. "I'm doing fine, M'dear. Every day I'm getting just a bit stronger."

"You're not going back to that stuff are you, boy?" Lucille's voice quavered. In the first year that she asked the question, it was more of an order than a question. Over the years it had turned into a request, and now it was a plea. Please, and I'm praying for you, were wrapped all around her query.

Ranger heard it all, and smiled more deeply, glad to have the right answer. "No, M'dear. I'm not going back to that stuff. I think if someone was to put some in front of me right now, I think I'd just tell them to get it out my face. I might even kick their ass, excuse me, M'dear, kick their behind, for offering. But I'm pretty sure I'd leave it alone."

Lucille looked at him harshly, and found a touch of razor for her voice, "Pretty sure ain't all the way there, son."

"M'dear, some things you just don't know until you're faced with them. You don't know how you'll be when you first be loving a woman. You don't know how you'll be when you first have somebody pointing a gun at you and you know they want to kill you. You don't know much, but you know yourself a little bit. So you can be pretty sure. And that's all you can be, pretty sure. But, M'dear, what fool would give all this up?"

Lucille didn't say anything. He had given up Jamal and Jeannine. He had given up a good job. He had given up so much. How was she to know what he would do now? Instead of answering, she changed the subject. "Well, I have some good news. They finally broke ground on that empty lot by Eddy. They say they're going to put some family homes there. I think the neighborhood is going to come on back. What you think, Elliott?"

"They are putting apartment buildings in, Mama. And you can be sure none of our folks are going to be there."

"Of course we'll be there, Elliott. We are everywhere now. They took this from us—of course we're going to get some of it back."

Sketch snorted. Lucille turned her head sharply. "You have a problem with something I said, Jamal?"

"No, M'dear. I just think they don't want us to have nothing..."

Lucille spoke softly, "But Jamal, we were brought over as slaves. We've never been given anything except a hard row to hoe. Everything we've gotten we had to take. We took back our freedom, I think we can take back a piece of our neighborhood. Don't you, boy?"

"Yes, M'dear, just like you say." And he quoted one of his mother's favorite sayings, "*Just look where you want to go and then go there.*"

For a few minutes, Jamal drew, and the room was silent except for the sound of the chalk scraping against the woven paper. He filled in the eyes, and had the arms and one leg perfectly detailed when his father sat up. "Taking a break for real now, son. Don't worry—you've got a few more minutes coming. Just a break."

Ranger sat back in the chair and stretched out his legs. He turned to his mother, who had settled on the sofa next to Jamal. "What about all the vegetables that are there?"

"In the lot? I guess folks are going to find somewhere else to plant. Lydia is just going across the way, she already told me. I don't know where those Vietnamese are going to plant. I was surprised when I first saw one of them over here. But they sure do know how to grow their funny-style greens."

Ranger shook his head. "That's the block the Franklins used to live in. Remember, M'dear?"

"No, I don't think I do."

"You know my friend Terry. Real moon-faced, and always ready to eat another four or five biscuits you cooked."

"Oh, yes," Lucille smiled, "Dinner Bell. Isn't that what your father used to call him?" Dinner Bell Terry Franklin. Always knew when it was time to eat."

"That's him. You know, first thing I saw when I got back here was a big hole in the ground where Terry's house used to be. I mean it looked like a bomb had come and cleared out the whole center of Fillmore. You would have thought that with all the time I spent over there, I'd have been used to seeing flattened-out land. You think you leave it behind, you think that's gone, especially coming home to the Panthers, and Black Power"

Jamal piped in, "Mgawah."

And then the two of them rang out laughing, "Black Powah."

"Black Power meant something then, you could see it, feel it. Jamal, I was in the hospital for a taste when I got home, and I was busy reading the newspaper and watching the news, and I was ready. I tell you, I was ready to join up with the home front, buy my black leather jacket, and bring all my military experience. I was ready! Then I got home and took the bus from the station..."

Lucille cut in, "We would have come and gotten you."

"I know that, M'dear. But I wanted to come into home on my terms, to walk through it, to see it, smell it, be there. To see who I knew, walking up the blocks. I had seen those streets in my mind when I was gone. I mean sometimes thinking about what it would be like getting home and walking the blocks and high-fiving all my friends, M'dear, that was what got me through. I just wanted to come on home at my own pace, in my own way, because I knew I wasn't the same as I was when I left. I came back grown. I had seen death in all its cruelty and mercy. And I had killed, more than once, more than I know. I tell you, I was ready for anything, that's what I thought. But I wasn't ready. I thought I was, but I was already on my way to being a fool. Fronting like I was more than I was, like I understood things I couldn't hardly even bear to look at or remember.

"I walked up and down that street looking for the places I used to know. The movie theater was gone, the blues house was gone, and the motorcycle club...

Jamal cut in, "They had a motorcycle club in the hood? What—the Black Hell's Angels?"

"No, boy. The Hell's Angels were killers. They didn't

want to do nothing but get drunk and tussle. The Rattlers, hey, they were the lovers. Modern black cowboys of the wild west, riding bikes instead of breaking broncos."

Lucille cut in, "See now, that's how you got yourself in trouble. Always thinking there's something special in that fast life."

"Mama, it was special. It was ours. Our own little beat, our own kinda walk. It was special. Maybe it wasn't always right, but I swear it was always special. It was ours. But when I got home, home was gone. Demolished. Nothing was left but empty lots and weeds. Lots of anise all through the street, so you could just smell licorice on the wind. But Mama, Fillmore was gone.

"I came in just past supper and it was already dark, but still early. Well, the first person I run into is Sliders. You know old mean Sliders. Well, he had skipped the Nam on account of prison, some kind of robbery beef."

"Elliott, are you talking about the Samuels boy, Jefferson? If so, that wasn't just stealing. It was armed robbery, and he almost killed somebody."

Ranger brushed her off, "Yeah, M'dear. Jefferson Samuels, Sliders. Anyways, Sliders asked me to come and have a welcome-home drink. So I say, cool. It wasn't as if you were expecting me."

"We should have been," Lucille cut in.

Ranger ignored her and continued his story, "Well, I'm thinking we're going to a club, but instead he hits the corner store, buys a bottle, and then walks over to the lot where Terry's house used to be. Then I remember that's the corner his auntie lived on, too. You know he used to spend a lot of time at his auntie's house, what with his father whipping his ass about every other day. Excuse me, Mama.

"So we go on in, squat down in the far corner, and pour out a swallow for those who went before. Then we start to drinking, and smoking, and catching up."

"Smoking what, Elliott?"

"Smoking smokes, Mama. Well, I'm sitting there and who should come up but Shortstop, that's Robert, Terry's youngest brother. Well, here he comes, all five foot eight of him, buff and clean as can be, strutting like the rooster in the farmyard, laughing and giving me a hug, but not easing up on talking all kinda mess, about how much a man he was, and what he could do, and where he'd been since the last time he saw me. That was when I realized he wasn't really talking to me, he was busy signifying about some kind of conversation that he and Sliders had had some other time. Well, Sliders jumps up off the ground, pulls a pistol from his pocket, and starts to pistol-whipping the man for what appeared to be no reason at all. So Shortstop, I mean Robert, is bloody by the time I get Sliders all the way off of him."

"Elliott, didn't that Jefferson boy die just after you came back? He was the oldest, as I recall. I was sick and couldn't make the service. Poor Esther. That was one mean man. Had the mean beat all the way through him. Even his mother said he died just from being so mean. Such a shame."

"He died of asthma, M'dear. But, I tell you, he probably needed to go on and die. He always was one to just want to jump on someone and start whupping them upside the head because he didn't like how they looked. They didn't even have to say something to him, just had to look what he called 'wrong.' Sliders was as crazy as they come. I saw plenty like him in the Nam. So of course, when I get home he was one of the first ones up in my face, just to show me I hadn't missed all I thought I had missed, and we hadn't come as far as I thought we had come.

"But like you said, Mama, he died just a few days after that. All of us who were home and still alive went to the service, even old Shortstop."

"The man he pistol-whipped? Why'd he go to the funeral, Dad?" Jamal asked.

"That's what I'm trying to tell you. The service was way too long, this song and that, and everyone telling all kind of lies about how noble Shortstop was. I mean he was an alright kind of guy, had some heart, but he sure wasn't a choirboy. About the only thing I know he didn't do or want to do was steal purses from old ladies. But you would have thought he was actually a kind gentleman, the way they talked."

"There's no reason to speak ill of the dead, Elliott," Lucille admonished her son.

"There's no reason to lie neither. Anyway, everything was finally said, and we all got up row by row to go past the casket one last time. So Shortstop, he ends up in the line about two, three people in front of me. Well, when he gets to the man, he just balls up his fist and fires on Sliders. Just hauls off and punches the corpse, yelling out, "Get up now, MF!"

"Elliott," Lucille reprimanded.

"Excuse me, M'dear, but that's what he said, 'Go on, get your sorry ass up now!'"

Now Hoodoo was just in back of me. He and I ran up and start to pulling Shortstop off of a damn dead man. You have to tell me the point in what he was doing. You can imagine the row. Sliders's sister started to screaming. His mama about turned blue. His youngest brother was sputtering, talking about who he was fixing to kill. I'm holding one arm of this crazy man, and Hoodoo's got his right arm thrown around blood's neck and got the other arm pulling on his waist, and here comes Sliders's sister, looking fine as the day is long trying to lay a couple of punches on Shortstop herself. I don't know if I should let her and then go on and cop some digits, or defend the brother who was all the way wrong."

"Elliott, that was a funeral. I know you showed some good sense." Lucille was laughing despite herself.

"Well, M'dear, I did not tell that girl to wear that tight dress with them round hips to her brother's funeral. But I did keep my mind on the subject at hand. One week home, and I was thick in the mix. But it wasn't so much like home, as it was sick and crazy, like all the stuff I'd just left."

Moments before, both Jamal and Lucille had been

laughing at the story, but now they both quieted, as a shadow slid across the room.

"Mama, you got any beer in the fridge?"

"Ranger, I thought you weren't supposed to drink when you're in a program."

"That's right, Mama. But I tell you what, I'm not doing no more kind of cocaine, no kind of smack, no kind of narcotics again. But I'm going to drink my brews, and I'm going to smoke my smoke."

"Elliott."

"Mama, don't worry. I'm going to run out and be right back."

Jamal stood up in anger. "You said you'd sit. I'm almost done. Come on, Dad, just another while and I'll go with you."

"I don't need an escort to the corner store, boy, and I'll be right back and sit some more, half the night if you need it, which I know you won't." Ranger smiled broadly, walking over and seeing the progress that Sketch had already made on the picture.

"Not bad, boy, not bad at all. Just give me ten minutes."

"Yeah, right." Jamal stood up, turned his back to his father with disgust, and walked out of the room.

Ranger called after Jamal, "Yeah, right. Catch you in a few. If I'm not here, you come and get me. But I'll be back. Have a little faith, Jamal."

Ranger walked over to his mother and sat next to her. She reached up and gave his shoulder a squeeze, "I'm sorry your coming home was so tough, son."

"It wasn't you, Mama. Come to think of it, wasn't that a Friday, too? I believe you took some fried chicken out of the fridge for me that night, and cooked some fried potatoes fresh."

"You and your father always argued about that, fried or mashed potatoes."

"And he won most of the time, but not that night. Not coming home. Mama, it didn't have nothing to do with you.

Coming home is always coming home. Easy, hard, it's just coming home." He leaned over and hugged her. He clung to her for a moment, and then let go whispering in her ear, "I love you, Mama. Thank you for dinner, and for Jamal." Before she could answer he stood up and walked into the foyer, calling back over his shoulder, "I'll be back in fifteen. Tell Jamal to just be cool."

Lucille had tears in her eyes. "All right, Elliott, I'll wait up for you."

"You won't wait up, you'll *be* up. I'm going to be right back. I love you, Mama."

And with that Ranger opened the door and walked out into the cool San Francisco summer night.

7. War Babies

i weave a dress of tears
pull warp threads through
the eyes of madness
silk soft strokes
my skin unraveling at its hem
dropping as dew to the sludge
of war's prelude.

we all have boy babies now.
womb deep they grow strong
push down in waves that
oppress gravity.
boys screaming even as they slide
from between blood-stained thighs
tearless sucking desperately.

the old women nod, finger prayer shawls
smile across stained teeth, "boys, it means war."
we all have boy babies these days, these times

i weave my dress in golden brown
toes catch at its hem
i trip over the tears
that lie across my breast
and glisten next to my womb and death.

It was that quiet time of night, that period when sleep opens its mouth and begins to swallow the edges of the city. Few cars passed the three-story corner house where Dawa sat, folding freshly washed clothes and placing them in piles on the bed. Dawa reached up and pulled loose the twine that held the weight of her henna-tipped dreadlocks into a tight pony tail. She sighed deeply as her hair fell around her shoulders. Her apartment filled the front part of the flat. She looked down from her third-floor bay window and saw Divisadero Street stretching out in front of her. Across the street, jazz was still drifting out the doors of the supper club, which in its latest transformation served African food and light jazz to packed houses. She felt a tired pinch in her neck and back as she stretched out her arms and listened. Tonight the doors were closed so there was no plaintive saxophone wailing, drifting in through the windows. Instead there was the sound of cars outside pushing the wind as they seemed to race to make the corner stoplight. An electric bus wire crackled from down the block, a woman's high heels chipped into the sidewalk, still moving in the rush-hour march that for most had ended hours earlier. But it was the short bursts of gunfire, the line of rat-a-tat-tats followed by moments of silence, and then a single bullet, sounding a weak and impotent response to the earlier barrage, that made Dawa pause and run her hand over her rounded belly. The baby inside turned over and poked out an elbow. She looked out the window to the street below that rustled in its half-sleep, the few street lights muted against the fog, the heeled footsteps already around the corner and out of hearing distance. The gunplay began again and Dawa sighed, stood up, and moved towards the phone.

Ruben walked in and stood next to her. He reached his

arm around her and pulled her close, "Sounds like the boys playing wild, wild west again tonight, baby."

"You've got some keen hearing, Ruben, to know it's not the girls. Or are you finally using some of those latent psychic talents?" she smilingly shot back.

Ruben smiled, "No, I leave all that heebie-jeebie information from the cosmos stuff to you and your cronies. I was just talking the odds, woman. Need some help folding the clothes?"

Dawa returned to the mound of clothing that filled the bed and nodded as she picked up a large tee-shirt, "Should I call again?" Again meant like she had done three nights before, and the night before that, and the week before that, too. Dawa was beginning to feel about calling the way she had often felt about going to church, like whoever she wanted to hear her prayers wasn't in that place, and whatever request she was making couldn't be answered inside those walls. Although she had stopped going to church, declaring that she was only going to pray in groups for a group purpose, she kept calling the station house, defending her actions by proclaiming she was going to "damn well make the police do the job they were paid to do instead of harassing regular people." Lately, though, she had begun to feel that it was absurd. She was just another blip in a database program. She rarely heard sirens after her call, or saw flashing police lights out of the window. News programs rarely mentioned the previous night's violence on the blocks, no newspapers ever added the statistics of this one wounded or that one killed. The absence of news was like the fog, a thick white blanket that hid all the city's miseries each night, and reflected only streetlights and moonlight, in glowing circles that made everything seem like a storybook setting. Even the projects looked serene, washed in the softness of an evening's mist. This, after all, was the jewel of the bay, the promise of the Golden Gate.

"You know they already hear it, Dawa. Hell, the station

is in the direction of the shots. No sirens though. But then it's only us shooting us," Ruben spat out. As he finished his sentence Dawa reached over him to the phone, "Woman, you know you were going to call anyway. Why do you ask me anything?"

Dawa stood up. "At least I'll go on record." She pushed an automatic dial button that rang through to the Northern police station. She wondered ruefully if there was a script in front of the phone that the duty officer read from. The lines were always they same. *Yes, the shooting was just a moment ago... No, she couldn't see where it was coming from... How could she possibly know how many people, she was inside, a couple of blocks away... Yes, she understood that a patrol car was already on its way... Of course there was nothing to worry about. Yes, just to be on the safe side,* wherever that was, *she would stay inside.* Dawa hung up the phone, her words heating as the receiver collided with the base. "Nothing to worry about. They're shooting up my neighborhood and there's nothing to worry about. They have it under control? What cartoon do they live in."

"Mighty-Mouse Dawa, Mighty-Fuckin-Mouse."

"Yeah, right, make the rodent the hero, and make the cat that keeps the home front halfway cool the villain."

Ruben moved towards Dawa and put his arms around her. She rested her head on his shoulder and shuddered as the guns went off again; this time a heavier revolver had joined the earlier pea-shooter. Then another semi-automatic joined the fray as the two minute skirmish intensified, and then, with the distant yelling of voices, ended. A moment of silence was broken by the squealing of car tires, more yelling, and then, finally, the sirens. First a police-car siren and then, a few moments later, an ambulance, with its piercing siren rising and falling, rode down the blocks past their corner and turned.

For a few moments the streets were totally silent. Then there was a rush of more sirens and some screeching tires.

Dawa gasped, "Ruben. I knew someone was shot." Her heart was beating fast and sweat was forming on the short hairs at the back of her neck.

"Baby, those are drug wars. It wasn't anyone we know."

"Oh, that's the same acute hearing that told you only boys were involved, I suppose."

" No, Dawa, it's the same odds. Dawa, the war's out there. Not in here. Let's fold the clothes and get to bed. We've got a lot of work tomorrow. We need to leave anyway."

"Ruben, they're shooting everywhere. I'll just have another phone number to learn and different officers to curse at."

"Dawa, it'll be better."

"Ruben, you know I don't believe that. It'll be different. And maybe they'll be a few more blocks between the gunshots and us. But Ruben, how in the hell is it going to get better?"

Ruben was tall and thin. Chocolate skin, a broad nose, full fleshy lips that stuck out in sharp contrast to his long thin cheeks and sharp chin. His eyes were small, but intense. He sat next to Dawa in silence for a moment. The woman who was always ready to be in charge, always sure of which way to go and how to get there, was lost in her thoughts. As she folded the clothes, Ruben could see her open, vulnerable and afraid. Her walnut skin showed deep shadows under her eyes. Small lines had begun to develop around the corners of her full-lipped mouth, and her forehead was full of deep frown lines. He reached out and stroked her face. "Dawa, if it doesn't work, we can always come back."

"It's not leaving or coming back, Ruben. Ruben, why are we bringing a baby into this? Another warrior for the cause?"

Dawa sighed again and picked up a pair of jeans and began smoothing her hand down the seams. She had thought it would be different here. She had been the holdout, and Ruben had held out with her, telling her over and over it was only love for her that kept him there. He had finally almost convinced her to move to Oakland before the baby came. They could get a larger place and have a yard for the coming child. Still, as Dawa sat on the edge of the bed folding the clothes, her eyes were full of tears, and her mouth was full of salt.

Dawa, whose mother had named her Cheryl after her great-aunt, had been the youngest of four when her parents had packed her, along with her two brothers her older sister, into the back of their Rambler station wagon and driven, suitcases piled on top of the car, and haul trailer full of furniture at the back, through the heavy dry heat of that Texas summer to the cool fog-filled wonders of the Golden Gate.

She should have known, Dawa had told Ruben two months earlier on that long night when she cried in his arms, she should have known that it was all a fake. Two nights after they got there, Dawa's father had loaded the family back into the car to go and see the Golden Gate Bridge. In retrospect, Dawa thought, when she first saw that the bridge wasn't gold at all, but a bright garish orange, it should have told her something. But the way the waves glistened across the water, and the small sailboats that sat like little puffs of cotton drifting across the water, and the hills everywhere, big hills, and steep hills, and round soft cloud hills rising out from everywhere ringing the Bay made her ignore all the early warnings. It was just like the picture postcards her Aunt Joline had sent to her three and four times a year since she had learned how to read. Just like the postcards, only better, cleaner, clearer, and full of sounds. There were fog horns that would push into your dreams in the middle of the night, cutting wedges in the walls of fog for the ships seeking safe harbor. And when Dawa stood on the edge of the Pacific Ocean for the first time, she thought that she was going to be swept up into the smooth waves in their thickness of blue, quietly lapping her toes with icy foam and seeming as close to peaceful as she ever again knew it to be. When Dawa saw the white-tipped waves, she was sure that if she rode out on a boat to the place where the sky curved around the water, and they touched each other, she would just fall off the edge of the world into an outer space of stars and comets and never stop floating. She didn't care that the Golden Gate wasn't golden. She didn't care that there was no backyard, and only steep steps leading up to a porch you couldn't really sit on. She even stopped caring that they had left their setter, Griff, with the neighbors, because San Francisco wasn't really a good place for a dog like Griff, that needed to run free.

From the beginning, Dawa loved the place as much as her sister Elise hated it. She thought it so much prettier than Texas. She loved the hills her mother always complained about. When her sister Elise took her to the park, she would go to the top of the hill and then lie down and roll to the bottom, arms stretched high overhead, the corners of grass and dandelion spurs catching on her lips. Then she would pull herself back up to the top, just to lie down on her side and roll down again, laughing and giggling at each bump in the long grassy expanse. But she should have known, she kept repeating to Ruben that night two months before, that night when she finally agreed to leave, she should have known from that first summer when instead of the dry still heat of Austin, and the pale blue sky, there was a morning and evening gray painted with a thick flat brush across the sky, she should have known that there wasn't really enough room in the city for her and hers.

She spent her first five summers in San Francisco wrapped in sweaters and thick socks. On the rare sunny two or three days they called a heat wave in the city, she would laugh as her friends complained about the heat, "You ain't never seen hot. Why, in Texas it gets so hot the cows sweat, and the white people turn bright red and have to wear ice packs just to keep working. Why, in Texas it gets, oh a hundred and ten, a hundred and twenty almost every day. Why, in Texas..."

Whenever she'd start lying, although Dawa never called it lying, she always called it *explaining so you get it all the way*, her friend Sara would pinch her arm real hard. "Wake up, girl. We ain't in Texas and it don't get that hot there. I know cause my grandma comes from there, and she told me."

"Well, you ain't never been there, so you don't know!" Cheryl would sass back and walk away mumbling to herself, "At least it was a real summer instead of the beginning of winter on the fourth of July."

Yes, she should have known that whatever her parents came here to find wasn't inside San Francisco. Her mother always swore it was better here, that it had been a good move. Her father and mother had followed Uncle Lester and Aunt Lynette, who had come to work in the shipyards. Her Aunt Joline had come separately and worked as a stock clerk in one of the major department stores. All of them had spent years writing and calling Dawa's parents to tell them to come out to California where the living was easier and the opportunity broader. Finally, her parents decided they were tired of knocking heads in Texas, and came to California. After a few years, all the family was able to chip in together and buy a pair of flats on the edge of the Western Addition. After that, Uncle Lester had actually left the docks and opened a barbecue restaurant called the Rib Pit, which catered to all the Texans that had migrated to the area and missed their own flavor of thick, biting, brown barbecue sauce, and enjoyed the particular way Lester had learned from his grandfather to boil the fat off and then slowly smoke the ribs. When he made enough money, he left the lower flat that he and Aunt Lynette shared with their twin daughters, Alice and Amy, and one undersized son, Samuel, and moved his family out of Fillmore and over to Bayview, where, as Lester was fond of saying, the sun shined more often, and you could walk for blocks and blocks and never see no kind of white people. Dawa's father said his brother was a "race man," which meant, as Cheryl then understood it, that if you were colored, you were right. Dawa's mother agreed that he was definitely racing, but said it wasn't all about color. Seemed like most of the time he was racing away from his home, either to work or to some other woman's arms. Her mother actually would say hussy, because any woman who messed around with a married man was definitely a hussy, and usually a whole lot worse, or else he was racing to some kind of liquor bottle, whichever he could get to fastest. Whatever —color, liquor, or women—he was definitely a racing man.

Dawa remembered growing up as a kaleidoscope of sounds, and tastes, and people. You could travel the globe and still be in the inside of San Francisco. If you went east, towards the Bay, you could ride on your bus ticket to China-well, Stockton Street and Kearny Street— but it was China to Dawa. The streets smelled like soy sauce and raw fish and plum sauce. Signs were in Chinese, and English was the foreign language there. On the other hand, going deep into Mission would find you in Mexico, with fresh-baked pan dulce and the sounds of brass horns and the click of boot heels on the pavement and lots of Spanish. She rarely went to the Richmond District. That was when mostly white people lived there. White Russians, her aunt Joline had told her, weren't communist like the Red Russians. But the Red Russians weren't any more Red than the White Russians were white. They just "thought red," her aunt had explained. Some of the White Russians even claimed to be royalty, her aunt had said. Dawa didn't know. What she did know was that was one neighborhood where you could be sure of getting a nigger or two spat out at you by some red-faced pudgy white boy who couldn't run fast enough to avoid getting caught and getting his behind whipped by one of her brothers, so instead he would stand at or near the foot of his house, and then, when he saw them passing by, would run up the stairs and slam the door in back of himself and hold court in the window, sticking his tongue out and pulsing in bright sweaty red.

Of course, Fillmore, where she lived, was the place to be. Leonard's had the best barbecue, next to her Uncle's, but his was way across the city, and Leonard's was right there. Besides, sometimes Leonard would give her a corner of hot link with a corn muffin just because he saw her with her nose pushed up against the glass, breathing in the sauce smells. And then, of course, there was the Princess Theater with its high balcony and thick cushioned seats. And her mother's friend's dress shop, and the fish store full of Italians, loudly yelling their own language to each other, and then without taking a breath turning and speaking English to Dawa's mother, Lucille. There was one man who always teased her about the tight greasy braids she wore, but always gave her mother the freshest of fish.

In Texas there were Blacks, and Whites, and Mexicans. In San Francisco there was some of everything. She even had a Korean friend named Jackie in her first-grade class, although Dawa didn't really understand that there was a difference between Chinese and Korean. Jackie would get mad at her and start talking about some kind of war, but Dawa said the only war she knew about they fought the Japs, and Jackie would just shake her head and start speaking in Korean. Dawa was sure it was cursing, although the child swore it wasn't. Dawa had loved Chinese food, especially fried rice with the sweet corners of barbecued pork, and sweet and sour chicken with chunks of pineapple floating in a red syrup that covered all of the long perfect grains of rice her mother would pile on her plate. When Jackie brought kimchee from home, and offered her friend some of the spicy pickles at lunch, Dawa realized that Korea and China must be two very different places.

Dawa didn't think that San Francisco was that different from Texas in some ways. Mostly the black kids played with the black kids, and the white kids played with the white kids, and the other kids kind of sat with each other, or sat by themselves. Dawa played with anybody that could kick a kickball hard and straight, hit a tether ball until it burned the palms of your hand, or spike a volleyball across a net. And Dawa ran. She dashed everywhere. Walking was, for her, something that adults did. Walking, unless you had lots of bags or books to carry, was something you did only if you were tired, or sick, or really, really, really sad. Although when Dawa was that sad she would go up to her favorite hill in that grassy park, and spread her arms and run down the hill as fast as she could, swallowing all the air her lungs could catch until it pushed out the sad, and in its place left only sweat and panting breaths.

But Dawa's mother saw San Francisco as the most wonderful place on earth. She said it was a place people could be people. She loved to go to the store and try on six different dresses and then walk out without buying any, just because she could. She didn't mind going to restaurants and being waited on last, because sooner or later she always got served. There weren't lynchings here, she would say, and that alone was worth the price of the trip.

Dawa was the baby in the family, which meant she got some of everything from everybody, but most of it was left over. Jeannine always said that was what made her so spoiled, being the youngest and having people always giving her something hand-me-down or not she was always on the receiving end. Dawa said that's what made her fast, having to be ready to grab that extra serving of potatoes, or rush to get a good place on the couch, even though Ranger always pushed her off to the floor. Those early days of San Francisco were family days, where you belonged more to the people you lived with than to the streets. But they were good days, and loving her home made her love the city. She was twelve years old, and had just started bleeding that evening when she stood on the hill holding Elise's hand. "I'll never leave here. See the way the fog comes over the hill. You know what, Elise, I bet the rest of the city is gone. If you walked there wouldn't be nothing there. It's being rebuilt and cleaned up every night. It disappears and then just gets started all over."

Elise would always mumble in response, "That's stupid. You walk over there and there be blocks and blocks of all those same-looking ticky-tacky houses."

"Yeah, because by the time you get there it's been rebuilt under the fog. But right now when it rolls in like a big breath a smoke coming out a dragon's mouth, why it erases the old and makes everything new again. I like it here, even if it is too cold." Elise would always shake her head, "Not me. Soon as I get old enough I'm going to Los Angeles, or at least Oakland or Richmond, where they have lots of summer, and no fog and no hills."

"They have hills in Oakland."

"Not for black people, stupid."

Sometimes, when Elise called her stupid, Dawa would rare up and start pulling hair and get in a fight that she always lost. But most of the time Dawa didn't care—she knew it was Elise who was missing out. But that was then, when there was a Fillmore full of folks from Texas, and Louisiana, and Arkansas. Most came like her aunt and uncle during the war, trying to be free and black, and have a little bit more than their parents or grandparents ever really dreamed of having.

But that San Francisco was gone, Dawa sighed, just like the woods Ranger used to climb in had been replaced by rows and rows of flat-faced stucco apartment buildings and houses. The neighborhood had become beiges and grays instead of colliding colors and loud, insistent neighbors. The city that hung outside her window seemed to have fewer hills, fewer lights, and the fog never got as thick anymore. It never got quite heavy enough to wash the city clean. Dawa felt a yawn coming and stretched out her arms.

Ruben pushed the remaining clothes back into the basket that sat empty at the foot of the floor. "It's late, honey. Let's go to bed. We've got all day tomorrow."

"Ruben, somebody died tonight. I just know it."

"Dawa, somebody dies every night."

"It's not supposed to be like this."

Ruben pulled Dawa down next to him. "Maybe this one lived, baby. Maybe he lived, and he's glad, and he'll go into early retirement from gun slinging."

"No, Ruben. I don't think so."

Dawa smelled Ruben's hair full of coconut oil and salt. She felt his arms gently rubbing her shoulders, and she fell, half-dressed and totally exhausted, into a deep heavy sleep. Ruben moved the clothes off the bed and gently undressed Dawa. He pulled the covers over her and sat on the edge of the bed stroking her face.

8. Witness in Shadows

Victoria's Plaint

I am not talking to you.
It seems that way because
I am in front of you
and words are flowing,
full of froth and spit,
in your direction.

But these babblings
are for myself and, perhaps
the demon and angel
who haunt me.

She came to me when
I was barely a child—
narrow hallways, starched lace
stern lectures were
the legacy I was given,
and the crucifix, of course,
always nails
always blood.

It was she who saved me.
Sometimes she is a morning birdsong,
full of comfort and good tidings.
Sometimes she is a dripping faucet,
all chatter and spittle.

She talks to no one but me.
I talk to no one.
These words are not for you
who think you see me.

They are for me.
And any angel, any demon
that may hear them,
let them knit their teeth together
and be still.

It started off a strange morning, and into the evening nothing had changed. I got Victoria to stay in for a few hours, but soon as it's all the way dark that woman puts her coat back on and says it's time to go out, that there was something we're supposed to see. I tell her she's supposed to see the inside of her eyeballs, and I'm supposed to see whatever I please, and try to get her to go to bed. She ignores me and stands by the door in her long wool cape, just waiting for me. She can tell I'm way across the room looking out the back window. I give up and go with her. Soon as she opens the door I'm at her elbow. Well, no sooner than we reach the corner, who should be coming up the other way but Dawa and Ruben, all getting along and cooing at each other. Dawa sees Victoria, but Ruben, he doesn't. He's too busy looking after Dawa, who is leaning heavy on him and seems real tired. Well, Dawa smiles at Victoria, and that woman actually tips her head in response. I mean for Victoria that's tantamount to a whole line of trumpeters blasting out a proclamation. Dawa turns her head as we pass and smiles funny style, like she's achieved something because Victoria acknowledged her. I don't want to disappoint the young lady, but tomorrow Victoria is sure to be back to her same don't-see-and-won't-be-seen self.

Well, luckily that night was the perfect temperature, warm enough so that a heavy sweater would do. Victoria really is kind of frail, and it doesn't do her good to be out when the air is all damp and chilly like it gets in a San Francisco. But tonight the air's dry, and jasmine nectar laid on it spilling down the block and across the street from the yard that housed it.

As we walked up and down the blocks, Victoria didn't say a word. She seemed to be looking for something, or someone. I wanted to ask her, but she still wasn't really talking to me. After a while I couldn't hold my peace any more. "Victoria," I shouted in her ear. Now, I didn't mean to shout, but I was getting exasperated. Victoria answered calm as you please,

"There is no need to be rude. You know how I hate rudeness. I am right next to you."

Well, I don't have any teeth, but I know I sent my words biting into her eardrum, "What are we doing walking up and down these blocks, around these empty lots? I mean, don't you realize we are walking in circles?"

"I thought it was this morning. I was mistaken. It's tonight."

Now I'm not sure what she means. Does she thinks that it's morning now? Or does she thinks it's tomorrow morning? Or did she just figure out that it's dark outside, and has been dark for a while? Instead of stirring up more murky water, I just keep walking with her.

"Come to witness," she whispered after a few blocks. All day Victoria had known that tonight would be her time to come out and witness. It became more and more regular, her role as a witness of death. She fretted over it, but she could see the light leave and move on each time death settled. The last time, she had seen those two old men fight in that alley. They both had knives, and the one that did most of the killing was no more at fault than the one that did most of the dying. At least that was how I saw it. But no one saw Victoria see, and she wasn't there to tell stories, just to see. And like I already told you, not too many folks want to hear me when I talk.

Finally, after what seemed like hours of walking in number eight patterns around the neighborhood, Victoria drew in her breath and gasped. "Oh my." As Victoria turned the corner, she knew that it was time. She stilled herself and gathered a light around her until she felt herself as invisible. Now, right at that moment, I'm not going to say she was invisible, and I'm not going to say she wasn't. But the point is that Victoria was sure she was invisible and so she saw it all, and I got to say that this time for sure almost no one saw her. And those that did, it seemed like she meant them to see her.

When we turned down the corner we saw Ranger and Sketch. Ranger was standing outside of one of the trouble grocery stores. Now, where we are, some of the stores, they are just stores, and some of the stores, why, they are like crab baskets pulling in all kind of scavengers off the streets. This particular store always had a crowd. Four or six young men, a young woman or two, often a police car. Tonight, there were three young men lounged all over the stairs next to the store, and another leaning on the wall in front of the boarded-up window. Sketch was just turning the corner, looking for his father.

Now, tell you true, I think the hunger came on Ranger, and he just had to go and feed himself. I'd seen plenty of times, seen the snow queen just reach out her long fingers and picked him up out the chair of his mother's house where he'd been sitting watching television with Sketch. "Going to get some brew, boy," and then he'd hardly turn around as he hurried out the door. But Victoria, she doesn't agree with me. She says it was the light pulled him out of the house and not that old rock. Well, I guess nobody but him can tell what it really was, and I haven't met up on Ranger walking these streets since he passed. No, not since that night at the anything-you-want, all-night-long store. And I do mean anything, anything you wanted, fast food, strong liquor, an assortment of drugs, kinky sex, or all kinds of guns. If you had money to spend, this was the place to spend it. Everyone knew the businesses that the store promoted. The clientele knew, the neighbors knew, the police knew. Hell, everyone knew. But as far as I could tell, except for a few grumbles here and there, nobody seemed to care all that much.

Yes, this was the store where the deals got made, inside and out. The store that was always open for some kind of business. The store that seemed to always have police cars in front of it, but never was busted. Fights didn't last long outside of the store. Usually K.C. came out with his shotgun and chased away any who he called troublemakers. Troublemakers was anyone who stopped folks from coming in and out of his store. As long as the commerce was steady, K.C. minded his own business. He and the outdoor entrepreneurs had an understanding. They kept the peace, and he kept his eyes from seeing what there wasn't no call to see.

It seemed like as soon as we spotted Ranger, Victoria knew there was going to be a problem. I don't know how she could see it, I mean usually she was so focused on not being seen that she only saw corners of what was going on in the street. Unless she was sitting still in the park, or resting on a bus bench, she never saw more than a flash of stuff herself. But this evening she saw everything just right before it was happening.

Ranger was nodding his head in a firm no to the man. He had a small bag of groceries in his hand. He was talking to that silly man, the one that keeps his hair all greased up and curled and calls himself D'Prince. The Prince of Death and Destruction, that's who he was. I bet he thinks he loves his mother, too. Well, he should of been the one. Everyone said he was the one they were really after, but you know sometimes things don't go the way they should go. Then again, of course, everything that happens, there's always a why and a wherefore. Well, I saw Sketch smiling when he saw his father coming out the store. But then he held back a minute and watched, looking for something to be passed palm to palm. Instead Sketch saw his father nodding no and moving away. Sketch started laughing. His father was going to make it through this night. Sketch realized that Ranger had seen him too when his father put on his walk and dipped into the wind.

"Pops is on tonight," Sketch yelled down the block just as a car rounded the corner and started spouting firecrackers out the window. At least that's what it sounded like, a noisy barrage of little fireflies lighting up the night. Sketch dove to the ground, sheltered behind a staircase. It seemed like all the gunfire was coming from one direction except for somebody's puny revolver and finally K.C.'s echoing rifle. While I was watching, everything slowed down. It seemed like Ranger was frozen, like he didn't know to duck or run. He was just frozen in space, until D'Prince pulled him down to the ground. But by then it was too late. As soon as the shooting stopped, and the car squealed off up the street, Sketch ran out to see his father staggering towards him.

Victoria knew Ranger had been hit because she saw the light shatter like a water glass into the night's darkness, that's what she told me as we walked home. I did notice how he focused on Victoria for a moment. I knew for sure he was seeing her. She held his eyes for a minute, and he became even brighter. It was always that way, those that could see her seemed to bring the light closer to themselves. At least, that's what Victoria believed. Then he turned to Sketch, who was running down the street, a wrenching howl getting ready to break out of his chest.

A warning gurgled out from Ranger's chest, "Stay low, boy, stay low, follow Hoodoo! He'll get you out!" Sketch caught his father as he fell towards the ground. "Daddy, don't die! Daddy, don't die!" Sketch's face was covered with tears, and his shirt was bathed in blood. "Nothing but trouble here. Get on, Jamal. Leave me be. Get on," his father's voice rattled, getting weaker at the end. "Tell your grandmother I love her. And tell Dawa, too. Tell her sometimes you just can't get away... Jamal, Jamal, you the man now. Jamal, I love..."

Victoria told me that when that boy kneeled next to his father and wrapped his arms around him, he was trying to push the light back into Ranger. Victoria said that she saw Sketch just scooping up that light and pouring it into the dying man and sometimes he got some in.

Right then, three police cars pull on up and the men jump

out guns drawn and shouting orders before they even got a chance to look and see what's happening. It was clear to me that they had waited to get close till all the shooting stopped, so why were they acting like they was so high and mighty? Well, the first one out the car, he walks over to Jamal who is holding his father and crying, and K.C. is wrapping a blanket around the boy's shoulders and telling him to be strong. Well, does that damned fool officer take a minute to assess what's going on? No. He just takes charge. First thing he does is pull Jamal away from his father, and throw him face down onto the pavement. He puts a knee in Jamal's back, and yanks the boy's arms up and cuffs them spitting out, "Shot your nigger, huh? Don't look like he's gonna make it. But you never can tell. He needs to die and leave some air for some law-abiding folk."

Jamal tried to twist around. When the officer stood him up, Jamal spit into his face.

"See what I told you, Joe...they all punks need to be taught who's in charge. You'd think his partner about dying in his arms would give him some humility. But no." He jammed his nightstick into the boy's ribs. Jamal folded over on his side.

Joe stepped in and pulled Jamal out of Hank's grip, "Shit, man, that wasn't necessary."

"You sure as hell better not put that on the report. He assaulted me. Spit, talked about my mother, and swung. I did what I had to. Anyway, he probably winged one or two himself in this little battle. Just 'cause his boss got shot doesn't mean he wasn't in on the game."

"He doesn't have a gun. This is the same boy we stopped earlier today. Likes to do graffiti and run. Man, it wasn't necessary."

"I recognized him. All that means to me is that we already gave him a bunch of chances, and he didn't learn. He needed an ass-whipping, and I gave him a shorthand version. If he'd a been home like he should a been, wouldn't be no problem."

By that time, an ambulance had pulled up, and medics were working on Ranger. "Let me go with my father," Jamal screamed out, as his father was placed on the stretcher.

The policeman with the thin mustache stopped leading him towards the squad car. "That was your father? Damn. Maybe he'll make it. I've seen a whole lot of folks shot up real bad that make it through. They'll take him to county."

I could tell by Jamal's face that he knew that the chances of his father surviving went from a little bit of nothing to less than that. It seemed like he had holes all through him. What I couldn't understand was why Ranger hadn't moved when the shooting started. He'd a gotten hit for sure, but not like that.

I saw that Jamal was praying as hard as he had ever prayed in his life, "Don't die, Dad! Please don't die!" Some other officers were taking a report from the store owner, who made it clear that Sketch was not involved. The mustached one offered Sketch a ride to the hospital. Sketch looked at the officer and then turned away. Without a word he started to run in the direction the ambulance had gone. As he ran, he wept. Large heavy tears flowing down his face with each long stride, I could hear him crying into the darkness, "Don't leave me, Dad! Don't leave me here!"

Tell you true, I wanted to go with him. But that's when Victoria started to move on down the street. She was afraid she might be seen. Oh, she didn't say so, but I could tell by the way she walked. She walked quick, her feet not making a sound on the pavement, up the hill and back the way we had come.

I could feel the scared all around Victoria, like she thought someone was going to come and snatch her or something. But after a couple of blocks she slowed down. I knew she was feeling invisible again. Still, the way she looked this way and that, darting her eyes at every doorstep, I could tell she wasn't all the way sure.

I can tell you for sure that no one saw Victoria wind her

way home. Not the ambulance driver or his assistant, none of the police in the six cars that ended up blocking off traffic in both lanes. Not the young men in the car or the ones on the street, and not the neighbors peeking out of curtained windows as soon as the shooting stopped.

When we got home I asked her did she think anybody saw her. "No," she said. "All they saw, if they saw anything, which I doubt, was a flash of fine white silk threads tightly woven around themselves. Only light could get through those strands." At least that's what she hoped, but she had been afraid. Yet I knew no one had seen her. When Victoria fell asleep that night, she was confident of this, and so was I.

9. Daybreak

Now, like I said before, Dawa should have known what happened to her brother right off the bat. I mean, what's the point of all that meditation and centering, and all that funny praying she be doing, if when it really counts you go blind. But maybe I'm being unfair, I mean maybe carrying the baby blocked some of the knowing. I never carried one myself, so I don't know how it affects you. But that morning, Dawa woke up totally unaware that her world was not the same as it was when she fell asleep. I had gone upstairs to try and tell her. I had tried to talk to her before, but she never heard me. But I thought maybe, just maybe this morning. I mean she needed to know.

Well, Dawa came to just as the sun cracked through the two-inch gap between the shade pulled over the window and the peeling window sill. She looked like she had spent the night tossing and turning, waking up trembling from dreams she could not remember. I had drifted upstairs just after we got back, so I was there when the phone rang. Ruben had answered it and taken care not to wake Dawa. News that bad, Ruben decided, could wait at least until sunrise. Now that's about a fool man for you. I mean some things you wake a body up for. It wasn't gonna do that baby no harm his mama missing a few more hours of sleep. But Ruben spends too much time acting like he got to be some kind of a father to Dawa. Now, I saw Dawa stir like she felt Ruben get up and move into the other room. But then it seemed sleep just piled up on her and pressed her deeper into the bed like a thick heavy fog that she could not move through. I wonder if she even felt Ruben when he climbed back into their bed and slid his arms around her and cradled her as if she was a child.

She kinda sighed like she did, a real comfortable sigh. Then for the next few hours she slept deeply.

I could tell right off, that early morning was Dawa's special time. Everything was quiet, even the streets and the gunshots from the night before were far away. She moved into the kitchen and began to brew a pot of tea. She opened up the built-in china cabinet and smiled. I once heard her tell Ruben that it was the cabinets that had made her want to rent the place. The cabinets, and the gigantic bay window that faced due west, bringing afternoon sun all year long, and on windy days bringing in a corner of the scent of the Pacific. The cabinet doors were small panes of glass crossed by wood. The shelves were narrow, but high. It was as if the place was already partly furnished. There was an ironing board that came out of the wall, which although it needed a pad and cover, was sturdy. Not that Dawa needed an ironing board. For the first five years she lived there she had used it as a place to hold plants. In fact it wasn't until Mr. Must-have-a-pleat-in-the-front-of-his-pants Ruben Pressman came to live with her that she, or actually he, purchased the pad and cover and began using the board to iron.

The first time Dawa tried to introduce herself to Victoria Cheevers I could tell that she thought she was talking to a white woman. She had been on her best behavior that day, stopping only an instant, "Hello, My name is Dawa Everman. I moved in about three months ago." She had one of those I'm-going-to-make-you-talk-to-me respectful-like tones in her voice, mixed with a whole lot of humph. "I see you leaving and coming from time to time, so I thought we should meet because we're neighbors. I live on the top floor in 850A."

Victoria was shocked. Now, I had been telling her that Dawa could see her, but like I told you before, Victoria talks to me, but she sure doesn't want to hear what I have to say. So Victoria says, totally shocked, "Are you sure it is me that you have seen?"

Now, I know that Dawa runs on a short fuse, so I'm expecting her to say something rude to Victoria about posturing and pretending, but that little touch of Southern came right on out as she answered plain as could be, "Yes, ma'am." But I realized that was because right before she opened her mouth she noticed that Victoria's powder did not completely cover her neck, a neck that was tinted with cold. She saw how Victoria's hair was curling at the edges underneath the pressed-down 1920s flapper hat she was wearing. Now, I hadn't told her that before we left the house. I had noticed, and she would have paid attention to me if I had mentioned it. But I was in a tiff myself, and tired of her not paying mind to my ideas. So Dawa followed that neck, up to its kitchen and on to the nose. Now, Victoria's nose is quite thin, and a bit too long to make the face truly pretty, but her lips, her lips are too full to come from anywhere but Africa. That's what I'm always trying to tell her, but she won't hear it. Well, anyway, Dawa just starts smiling, "You're colored, just like me. You're black."

Victoria looked at Dawa's hand which still hung outstretched in the air and was so shocked that she started talking mid-sentence, hoping to distract her young neighbor. "...Victoria Cheevers. I know you rent from my niece, Sheila. My family has lived in this building for over a hundred years. We are not common, and we do not rent to common people."

Dawa opened her mouth and threw back her head as she laughed, "Well, you ask any of my friends, Mrs. Cheevers, and they'll testify that I am anything but common."

Before Dawa could get her sentence out, the woman had turned on her heel and was rushing down the street muttering to me, "I don't know how she can see me. No, I have not been loud. You always have something to say, but none of it is right." I spoke up and pointed out how I had been trying to tell her that but she just cut me off. "You don't have to yell in my ear. Maybe she just thinks she's seen me before. Lots of people dress in white. I mean I'm not the only person that understands the light. I know what you are going to say, but I am not afraid. I just do not like being seen. Well, she said she was not common. Yes, I know what I have said about women who laugh loud like that and don't even have the decency to cover their mouths, but she seems kind. Well, what do you know about kind?" I knew this was a time to keep quiet, so I did. I just turned around and saw Dawa standing there with her mouth hanging open.

From that day on, I knew, Dawa would be determined to find out why this woman was crazy. Now, this child don't even comb her hair. She calls natural having those Medusa locks hanging down her neck, so you can imagine what she though of sweet Victoria all painted up like that. Some days Dawa would sit on the front step waiting for Victoria to emerge from the house. Most of her free daytime was on weekends, but it seemed that Victoria rarely came out on weekends, or in the evening, or, Dawa soon realized, at all. In fact, when Dawa asked the landlady about the old woman, Sheila Woodson shivered and didn't respond. Dawa pressed her, "I haven't seen your aunt lately."

"Of course you haven't." Sheila shivered again and rushed into the house.

Dawa started asking people about the woman. It's hard to miss a woman who is always wearing white and is painted in white from head to toe. The only time she would blend in would be Halloween. But people never seemed to see her, except Dawa's brother Ranger. He had talked to her. He said he'd ask her about the weather just to see her frown up and then turn and run. He'd hoot, "Ghost lady, looks like fog, you'll need a warmer cape than that!" as she scurried away. Ranger saw her all of the time, too. I always thought that was strange, him being in a haze so much of the time. I mean there was a time when he could walk past his own son on the street and not recognize him, but he always saw Miss Victoria.

By the time a week had passed, Dawa was a pro at finding

Victoria. She saw her early mornings in the alley, and evenings rushing across Golden Gate, and early mornings sitting in the mini-park. Why, I think I saw her smile when she looked down at Victoria that morning, but Victoria swears she was biting her lip. I don't think so, because I know Dawa was real surprised when Ruben walked into the room. She was turning the tea-filled mug in her hands and warming her palms when she saw him already standing in the doorway and gave a start. She even spilled some of the hot liquid on her robe.

Ruben moved towards Dawa and sat next to her. He took her hands in his and sighed, "Dawa, Honey, last night..." Then he held the words that burnt like lava on his tongue, knowing that there was no way to slow down their flow or soften their content. "Dawa, Sweetheart, it was Ranger."

"What was Ranger, Ruben?" But, as the words fell out of her mouth, Dawa knew, "Last night it was him, he..."

Ruben cut her off. "Your mother is probably home now. They had to sedate her at the hospital and were keeping her for observation. Elise was taking her home early this morning."

"Why didn't you wake me? Where do you come off deciding to keep news like that from me? Who in the hell do you think you are? My brother has been shot and you don't bother to wake me up!!! Who in the hell gave you the right to turn me into some kind of child, try to feed me pablum? Dammit, Ruben..."

"Dawa, not shot. He's dead. It was the middle of the night when the call came, and there was nothing you could do. Jamal is missing, too. No one has seen him since he went out to look for his father last night." Ruben paused as Dawa stared at him, and then continued, "You needed your rest and..."

Dawa started hitting Ruben and screaming. Suddenly all the knowing she had had inside since last night's moan of death came up inside of her, a thick bile of awareness. Words did not come out of her, only yelps and cries and wrenching tears. Ruben caught her arms and pressed them to her sides. He circled his arms around her and held her close. "Dawa, that's why I waited till morning. Your mother doesn't need to be around your explosions. Get it together and we'll go down there."

Dawa shook off his arms and rushed into the bathroom, washed hurriedly, and then dressed thoughtlessly. First she put on a pair of jeans and a sweatshirt that she had left out for packing day. Then she stopped for a minute, returned to her closet, and pulled out a long flowered skirt and white knit sweater.

When she finished dressing, she started wandering around the apartment. "Ruben, where did you hide my keys? Ruben, when I get back I hope you aren't here, because I'm not moving anywhere with you. You asshole. Where do you get off..."

She would sit down and then get back up and start rummaging through drawers and looking in the pockets of her clothes. "Okay. Okay, I'll leave without my keys. Where's some change for the bus? I need a dollar. Ruben? What am I talking about? I can walk. Need the walk, yeah, I can walk."

Ruben came close and tried to put his arms around her again. She hauled, swung her left arm out, and cuffed the side of his face. "Damn, Dawa." Dawa stopped and let her arms hang limply at her sides. She stood in the middle of the floor and began to cry in large halting hiccups of pain. Ruben went to the kitchen and got a glass of water for her and gingerly passed it to her, concerned that she would hit it out of his hand.

"Dawa, I called Jeannine and Mitch over. We'll all go to Lucille's place together. I called Elise and she said your mother is still asleep. I called the hospital and they'll need you to sign some papers. It seems that Elise told them that you were the one who handled all his affairs. I'm sorry, honey, but you were so tired, and I knew you'd need the sleep.

There wasn't anything you could do. Your mother didn't even know you weren't there. Elise told me she kept calling her by your name. Honey, there wasn't anything you could do."

Dawa didn't say a word. I saw her put her hand to her belly and feel the baby turn inside of her. It kicked softly and adjusted itself. I could tell that it was restless and could not find comfort inside its warm chamber. Dawa stared down at her hands. I noticed how they were shaped like Ranger's, wide palms, oversized for a woman, and thick fingers. Then she let Ruben put his arms around her and hold her. The two of them sat on the sofa saying nothing, rocking in the sadness of the morning.

10. Jeannine's Ranger

loving you
is riding a star

my fingers hot sparks
an avalanche crushing lungs
cutting dreams

loving you is
loose belly folds
flesh
damp moss
pressed to my nose.

That Saturday morning Mitch was about as hell-fire angry as Jeannine had ever seen him. He was hurrying to Dawa and Ruben's place, just racing to the red light and then slamming on the brake and cursing. Ruben had called and told him to tell Jeannine what had happened. As soon as she heard, early as it was, she hopped out of the bed, called Brenda to come on over and look after the children, took a half a bath, threw on some clothes, and rushed out the door all in about six and a half minutes. Still, there was Mitch yelling at her to "Come on!" and demanding to know why she was taking "so damn long." He drove down the hill, across the bridge, and all through Fillmore, like only one half of his brain was working, the half that said go. Then all of a sudden he jammed on the brake again and almost threw Jeannine into the windshield.

"What the hell's the matter with you, Mitch? You want to kill us too?"

"I almost hit that woman."

"What woman?"

Jeannine didn't see any woman, but she saw Mitch just sitting there, sweat popping out of his top lip and his hands clenched around the steering wheel. The car in back of them started honking the horn and Mitch just ignored them. "Mitch, we're holding up traffic," Jeannine called out. A car screeched around him, and the driver was yelling epithets out the window, talking about Mitch's mother, Jeannine, and everyone else. Mitch just sat there.

"Jeannine, how could you miss her? It was Dawa's white woman. The one she always talks about, all painted up in white. I almost hit her."

"Mitch, I didn't see anybody there."

Mitch eased off the clutch and moved through the intersection. He didn't say anything. He was scared. He got still when he was scared, and he would bite down on his teeth so that his lips went thin and hard. Now his forehead was sweating and he was looking straight in front of him. He was driving too slow, and stopping real long at each corner.

"Jeannine, are you sure you didn't see her?"

"No, Mitch. But Dawa says she's like that, can't be seen unless she wants to be seen."

"Well, I saw her today," Mitch mumbled. "I definitely saw her, and almost hit her pinched-up frame. That's all I would need, in jail for killing a crazy lady."

Mitch was usually the one that Jeannine could depend on in a crisis. He was the one who kept his head and moved just like a knife through soft butter, smooth and sure, spreading his calm around the place. So Jeannine was taken aback by his jerking driving and cursing. "All the crazy people come out on the front lines. It's always that way. And this is a goddamn war, a goddamn undeclared war," Mitch muttered, and then began to rush to the next red light.

That was just not Mitch. Mitch was one of those still-water-run-deep kind of men. Most people didn't take to him. Or more accurately, he didn't take to most people. He let very few get close, and the ones that did, well, he never let go of them. He didn't really do much more than tolerate Dawa. He found her "too damn loud, too opinionated, and she thinks her stuff is a whole lot hotter than it is." Jeannine always laughed at him and his attitude with Dawa, "I think you're just angry because you know Dawa doesn't really give a damn if you, or anyone else for that matter, likes her or not. I mean you take Dawa like she is, or you don't, and either way she's not going to get too ruffled. Sometimes I personally think she need to check it out and take heed of what people are saying, but Dawa she always says to me soon as I get the edge of that idea on my tongue, 'No, Jeannine, that's a personal problem. I can't do nuthin' about someone's personal problem.'" Not that Dawa and Mitch argue, at least anymore. As the years have passed, he has learned to be cordial with her. Whenever she came to visit, which was far too often as far as he was concerned, but in fact only a few times a year, Mitch would say his ten or so words, and then move into another room, if not all the way outside and down the block.

Mitch is solid, that's why Jeannine fell in love with him, because he was not like Ranger. Mitch managed to get in and out of Vietnam and hold onto the best part of himself, but Ranger got lost somewhere in there. Mitch seemed to have been able to push all that ugly into a locked-up corner of himself and go on. Maybe he was a little harder than he would have been, maybe a little colder, but the war never stopped Mitch from moving forward. It just slowed him down and changed his path and showed him what was really important to hold onto. That's what he told Jeannine. That's why, he would say, he held onto her and the children so tightly; too tightly sometimes, but he had a reason. As far as Jeannine was concerned Mitch had adjusted. Ranger never could stop looking back. Jeannine had always wondered who Ranger would have been if Vietnam hadn't curved through his intestines like some kind of parasite that wouldn't let go.

When Jeannine and Ranger first met, she knew he was of an age that he had either served in Vietnam or else in jail because he hadn't finished but two years of junior college. He wasn't the kind to try and hightail it to Canada, and seeing the way he liked to party, and only worked part-time jobs, he didn't seem like the type to be a draft resister either. She had asked him about it on their third date. He just snapped at Jeannine, "Been there, came back, it's over." She left it alone after that.

Months later she found out a little more. They were getting quite experienced at looping the loop with each other, taking up most of each other's off-work hours, and a whole lot of hours that Jeannine used to spend with her family. It was on a Wednesday afternoon, and he had the afternoon off. Jeannine had taken time off that day, just because she was so in love with looking at him smile at her, and really didn't care about that "tired old clerking job" at the hospital. They were walking through the farmer's market in downtown Oakland. She had grabbed a hold of his hand, and he, as usual, held hers real loose, like a warm, limp, banana peel.

Ranger was all mouth in public, but he rarely showed real affection. Behind closed doors, you couldn't find a man more expressive. He was always touching Jeannine and pulling her close and feeding her from his plate, but on the street, the most he liked to do was brush shoulders, or sometimes put his arm around her just for a moment, to show that they were still joined. It was like he didn't want strangers, especially any partners he might run into, to know how close they really were.

Now on that day, Jeannine really didn't care what he called his *privacy.* She wanted everyone to know that she had a man, and was planning on keeping him for the long haul. So she grabbed onto him and was pulling him towards a table that was stacked high with fresh greens. Just at that moment this full-faced slim Asian woman, nut brown and long dark hair, rushed up, eyes all full of tears, and starts going on to him in Vietnamese. And he just picks her up and gives her a long bear hug. Then, in this kind of stiff-tongued way, he answered her in her language. Jeannine could tell he was asking her questions, and she was answering, but he didn't seem to be sure of what he was hearing. Finally he asked her to speak English. "It's been too long. No need to remember here," he said. "Always, Elyeet, always there is a reason to remember," she smiled at him. His eyes were full of tears, but he didn't turn away. It was like Jeannine didn't exist.

"She moved North," the woman said, "She took Elyeet three and moved North because our aunt and uncle were still alive and had room in their home. They don't treat your son like enemy, they make him fourth son. I came here with my husband. You remember Dao. I asked her to come here and we find you. She did not want to come. She did not want to leave home."

Ranger just stood there without a word. Then he said very quietly, "She loved the land." It seemed like the whole market was full of noise and motion, people laughing and pushing each other around the fruit-and-vegetable stand; a man singing a half-block away, reaching his voice over the blocks, talking about "Golden sunshine, I want to go there...," a car on the street in front honking its horn, a rush of buses, but the three of them were caught in a hole without echoes, just dark with its silence. Just then Jeannine realized that Ranger was crying. The woman reached up and wiped away his tear. "It's okay, Elyeet. Too much time past. She stays home now with her new husband. She has one daughter and two other sons. Is this your wife? Very pretty, very good woman for you, Elyeet."

Ranger remembered that Jeannine was standing next to him, introduced the two women. "Mei Lei, this is Jeannine. Jeannine, Mei Lei. I was close to her family during the war."

"You call me Pookie," the woman smiled at me. "That's what Elyeet named me. Pookie. He says I'm just like his little sister, always poking my head where it doesn't belong. I was his little sister in my home."

Then Ranger, who just moments earlier had not even wanted to hold Jeannine's hand, pulled her as close as he could and held on like he thought he'd drop through the ground if he let go. "I need to write her, Mei Lei. I need to let her know more. If she needs help or anything, if you need help or anything..."

"You give me your address. I will write her and maybe she will write you."

Ranger just looked at Jeannine. She rummaged around her purse and found a piece of paper and wrote down his name and address, and phone number, and handed it to Mei Lei. She turned it in her hand, and then passed the paper back to Jeannine, "You write down your name too. She will want to know name of his good wife." It wasn't a request so much as a demand, so Jeannine took the paper back and wrote down her name, just her first name. They weren't married, but she didn't want to say so. Ranger hadn't corrected Mei Lei, and Jeannine definitely wasn't going to say anything she didn't need to say.

Then Mei Lei reached her hand up and put it on Ranger's cheek, "You always good man, Elyeet. You tried to help my family. We keep you in our hearts. It was sad time for everybody. Now it is better time. I will write that I saw you, Elyeet. Goodbye. Nice to meet you, Jeannine. Goodbye."

Then she turned and walked away. Ranger didn't say a word of explanation to Jeannine. He just turned towards the table of greens and started picking up bunches. He didn't stop till he had eight big bunches in a bag. Jeannine wasn't too happy about the prospect of washing and picking all of them, but she didn't say a word. He paid, and then they went back to her place, where she washed and picked, and washed and picked, while he put on some of her old Temptation records and just sat in a corner, looking at his hands, deep into the night. When he finally came to bed, he just held on to Jeannine and cried until he fell asleep. She didn't ask him any questions, and he didn't offer any explanations. It wasn't but a few weeks after that, he asked Jeannine to marry him and a couple of months after that, when a thick envelope arrived with a postmark of Ho Chi Minh City, and pictures of his five-year-old boy, and his boy's mother.

Jeannine was not altogether happy that Ranger got some conscience about the girl he'd been seeing. Even though she and Ranger were married, Jeannine knew it made a difference that he had a son by this woman. At the same time, Jeannine knew that if she had had somebody's baby in wartime, she would sure want them to come see about her and the baby, and probably wouldn't care how many years had passed.

Ranger showed her the pictures, and told Jeannine that he was shipped out before Mei Lei was even showing. He said he had meant to go back and get her, but when he got back stateside everything had changed so. He said that all the Afros and black is beautiful and Panthers made him just want to be about freeing Black people here. He told Jeannine how he wrote to Mei Lei for a while, trying to explain what was happening. He said she wrote back once with a picture of the baby. After one of his own letters came back, and then a second was returned, he stopped writing. He said he had always meant to go and find his son and his former lover. "I never married her," he would always tell Jeannine when she frowned up. "You are my only wife. First, last, and only." And then he'd hold her real close.

Still she worried. Jeannine was sure that there was a special kind of close you get surviving war together. But Ranger always said that he saw so much ugly over there that he spent most of his time forgetting, and that meant he had to forget the good moments along with the bad. He said he had gotten pretty good at pretending that almost two years of his life didn't really exist.

For a few years, Jeannine would see envelopes coming to the house every six months or so, and she knew that Ranger would send back money, and even sent photographs of her. But they never spoke of his other family. It was years before she found out that he had made visits to Mei Lei's family once a month, and had become godfather to her youngest son. That was before drugs and the streets had finally claimed him, and he was tearfully asked not to return anymore.

Jeannine made sure that she got pregnant as soon as could be. Ranger had wanted to name the baby after himself, but Jeannine said no. He already had a son with his name, and he wasn't going to have another. Ranger was real comfortable with that, so he asked about naming him after his father's best friend. Even though Elliott never saw him anymore, he still held deep abiding respect for the man. It was shortly after Jamal's birth that things started to break down.

About that time, Ranger had started arguing all the time.

He had taken to spending nights out, and refusing to answer any questions when he showed up back at the house. He cashed his checks before coming home, and brought less and less of the cash to Jeannine. She tried not to see it, but it was clear. She knew there was a problem. When he was home she was either breathing too loud, or not breathing loud enough and giving him the creeps with her quiet. Everything was reason for a fight, how Jeannine said something, or how she didn't tell him something else. It seemed like even Jamal getting ear infections or chicken pox was her fault.

Everything was falling apart, and Jeannine didn't really know why. Ranger was getting angrier and angrier all the time. Finally he decided that he wanted to try Jeannine out as his private punching bag. That was when she decided to think about calling it quits and moved back in with her father for three months. After promising to reform, Ranger agreed to go talk to somebody about whatever it was that was bothering him, and Jeannine returned home.

The night Jeannine came home, Ranger seemed so glad to see her and Jamal, but he wouldn't touch Jeannine. He hugged his son, and gave him a bath and put him to bed, after a little peck on the cheek as a hello and welcome back to his wife. She was so hurt. Jeannine thought they'd have one of those all-night making-up love sessions that make you almost not mind the arguing you did for the way you stretch and bend and fill up the sky with each other, but he wouldn't even come near her. It was as if he was afraid to touch her. He just kept thanking Jeannine for coming home. She fell asleep hearing him whisper it close to her ear one more time, "Thank you, sugar. Thank you..."

That night, Ranger had night sweats so bad that the damp in the sheets woke Jeannine. She shook him awake and made him help her change the sheets in the middle of the night. Jeannine was used to Ranger having night sweats. He would go in and out of them some times two or three weeks running, and then nothing for months. She had made him go to the doctor, but the doctor always said something about nerves and too much salt, and sent him home. This night though, she knew something was different. After the bed was all cool and clean, Ranger settled back in and pulled Jeannine close and made love. His touch was like slow, long tears. He was so soft and careful like he wanted to remember every corner of her in case he didn't wake up, like he wanted to tattoo her crevices on his fingertips and his tongue. He was gentle and trembling, and after they got swallowed in the waves, and then were washed back up, quiet and panting, all entwined with each other, he thanked her again for coming home and fell into a deep hard sleep. Jeannine fell asleep too, feeling happy and whole, and knowing everything would be alright.

Hours later when Ranger woke Jeannine up, he was sitting straight up in bed howling, tears rolling down his face. She sat up and threw her hands over his mouth to quiet him, so he wouldn't wake Jamal. Then he just fell to sobbing in her arms. Jeannine had never seen a man weep like that before. She had seen her daddy crying deep over her mother, after she passed from a vicious cancer that just ate her insides out, but it wasn't this kind of ragged and searing pain. There was no bottom to Ranger's sobs. Finally he quieted and began to talk to her.

"Jeannine, he was only maybe fourteen, fifteen. I mean he was the same age as my younger brother at the time. Maybe a little older. And I aimed my rifle almost point blank and shot out his middle. His eyes were so brown, and alive, and when that bullet hit him, I swear I heard him call out. Jeannine, when I saw the blood spreading everywhere, and felt his scream crawl down my back, you would have thought I had been hit, because I started screaming too. If Hoodoo hadn't grabbed a hold to my shirt, and pulled me down to the ground so I would roll back into the underbrush, I'd of been hit, too. First person I ever killed, and it was a hardly more than a child. Jeannine, hardly more than a child. What in the hell was I doing in somebody's else country killing their babies? Jeannine, I'm going to have to pay. You can't kill somebody's baby and not pay the price."

Jeannine didn't see his dilemma. After all, a the boy was armed and pointing a gun right at Ranger, who wasn't all that much more than a boy himself, which to her mind meant he had no choice. Jeannine's words cut through the dark, "Ranger, it was a war, for God's sake!"

"Yeah, I saw it that way at the time, but I'm not so sure now." Ranger said that if he'd a known what it was going to do to his soul, killing children and all, he would of let them kill him.

Well, Jeannine had enough of that. She pulled him out the bed and made him walk down the hall and look in their child's room. There was little Jamal sucking his middle two fingers and smiling in his sleep. "Ranger, look at him. You were supposed to have this child. You were supposed to have Elliott the third. No, maybe the war wasn't right, but you don't have to pay for holding onto your own life."

They walked back to bed and Ranger started talking about the war. He was like a geyser, water bursting out, strong and hot, telling her a piece of this story and a fragment of that one. He turned on his stomach and told her the story of how he got the scar on his right shoulder blade she had always asked him about. "I was winged, and starting to lose it, and then Hoodoo came and pulled me down, and saved me again. Told me he was gonna do it one more time and then my ass was my own to save. But Jeannine, he kept on being there, helping keep me together, teaching me, me, how to survive." Ranger said of Hoodoo that he came home too, missing half a leg, but home. But Hoodoo, he never was right again.

Ranger told Jeannine that Hoodoo was born with some kind of African power, and he used it all up staying alive, and killing, and killing some more, and keeping other people, like Ranger, alive. He said that when Hoodoo got home he was missing a big old piece of himself, and had been looking for it ever since. Ranger said Hoodoo got a silver star, and three bronzes, and a piece of plastic to replace his leg. "Seems like a raw deal to me."

Ranger said Hoodoo was struck near his kidney a different time while he was pulling his friend Ranger out of harm's way, and had a piece of shrapnel clipped off the corner of his ear. That night, Ranger kept going on about that boy he killed. He said he killed that boy, and maybe six or seven more. He said there's six he's sure of, one he thought he did by the way the man cried out, and another four or five he thinks he hit. He said he was always getting teased by the others who told him there was no way of telling who you really killed unless you were right up on him. Everyone that is but Hoodoo and Ranger. He said the two of them kept a tally, twenty-seven for sure. Ranger said, "That's more than the number of people I can give full names of in my own family." Of course, he curled his lip as he spoke. "You really don't ever know how many you kill. How could you know who lives, or who dies later, or how many were really in that bunker. We didn't always check. Mostly we were just firing scared, and they were firing back, just as scared. Then there's the mines, of course, you never know how many you get with the mines. You aren't even there when they hit," he said, and laughed in a real eerie way. "That's where we racked up lots of kills. Some of them our own. All kinds of friendly fire." Yeah, he said he kept track so he'd know how much sin he'd have to pay for when he got home.

Ranger told Jeannine that he knew from the first time he saw fire, he knew that he was going to make it home. He said that every time shooting started, the first thing that happened was his ears were full of the sound like one loud screech, and then in an instant all the sound stopped, and everything just moved in slow motion. He said he actually saw the fire come out of the gun, and then saw the bullet moving towards him, and then moved aside so he only got winged. Ranger said it was almost like you got into another time rhythm, and if you glided through that time there wasn't any sound, just movement. You just had to keep your eyes open and move in the spaces, like moving through a crowd on a downtown street without brushing up against anybody.

Ranger explained that, as far as he saw, there were just three kind of men in a war. There was the ones who panicked. They ran every which a way and made easy targets for the enemy. In fact, Ranger said they was as much the enemy as the ones who was shooting at you, because they got in the way and made the chaos even worse. Then there was the ones who froze, who just stood there and watched as people fell around them. They watched bullets go into their own insides, and watched the blood roll out, and didn't move, just screamed or wept and finally fell. And then he said there were the ones like him, that made it a dance, that found a rhythm in the gunfire and moved around and through it. He said it wasn't so much that he could slow down time as he could slow down himself, and move around time easy and careful so as to stay alive. From that first day when the war got real for him, Ranger said he always let things slow down while he caught his bearings, heard the bullets coming in ones and twos, and just kind of knew the ones that were headed his way. He said you either panic, freeze, or get still and quiet inside and change the way time moves around you, if you want to live through a war.

That night, as Ranger talked, he kept piling the ghosts of body after body of people he knew he killed, or people he thought he might have killed, or people he saw killed, or people he wanted to kill, on their bed. By the end, Jeannine was crying too. They were both weeping and wailing. Jamal woke up in the midst of the two of them blubbering away, and rushed into the bedroom. Of course, Ranger turned away. He didn't want to have his son see him crying. But the air in the room was so heavy. It was just full of all this sadness, but Jamal just climbed onto the bed and threw his arms around his daddy like he didn't notice a thing.

"Daddy, I'm thirsty and I'm scared," he whispered in

Ranger's ear. Ranger clung to the child like the boy was some kind of lifeboat. He hugged him tightly and then put him on his shoulders and carried him downstairs to get some water. After he tucked him back into bed, he returned to Jeannine, dry-eyed and exhausted. "Jeannine, I killed too many people. Too many people."

Jeannine tried to tell him that it's how he lives now that counts. But he just said something about no matter what, you can't erase the past of what you've been. "What about what you are, after all of that? Doesn't it count, Ranger?" He just ran his fingers down Jeannine's face, and then pulled her close and buried his lips in her hair. He pulled back and frowned, "Sometimes what you are after isn't enough, Jeannine, because you know there's nothing you can really do to make it all right." Then he started playfully kissing her all over her face, thanking her every third or fourth kiss, "Thank you for coming home, sugar. Thank you..."

Jeannine had thought that night would be a new beginning, that maybe now Ranger could get loose of all the ghosts that he carried around. But it seemed instead like that was the night he decided to join them. Within six months he had moved out of the house. Before a year passed Jeannine had taken to locking the door against his haphazard returns, sometimes with a few dollars and some groceries, sometimes with gray skin and sunken eyes and a need for a meal. That was the last night they were ever so close, and Ranger spent his remaining years running from that closeness.

As Jeannine remembered that night, she began to quietly weep. Mitch reached over and put his hand on Jeannine's knee. He saw the tears that were streaming down her face. "I thought you told me he killed all the love you had for him. Burnt it up in a crack pipe. What are all those tears for?"

"He's still the father of my child, Mitch. He just got swallowed up by all those monsters he carried inside of him."

"No, Jeannine, he got swallowed up by being too selfish to let that damn dope go. I mean everyone has some kind of pain. I've got my battle scars, too. I've got my stories and it's not all so easy for me. Hell, I'm raising his child and two of ours. So I really don't have too much damn sympathy."

"Mitch, you know better than that."

Mitch didn't say a word, just kept driving. When they reached the house, there was a parking place waiting right in front. "I guess Dawa's going to say she arranged this for us," he kind of sneered, and then he broke down and cried, too. "Jeannine, where's the end of it? We dying again just like before, friendly fire. That's what they call it you know, friendly fire." She knew better than to say anything. She just sat there and watched him pull himself together and put on his calm lake face and get out the car. The only way she knew he wasn't all the way back together was the way he tightly held onto her hand while they climbed the three long flights of stairs. As they walked, Jeannine's heel got caught on a step and broke off. Mitch halfway caught her before she slipped down about four or five steps. He started to yell about how he'd told her to throw out those damn shoes, and why in the hell was she dressed up anyway. Just then, Ruben opened the door.

Mitch's bellowing was certainly more effective than using the doorbell. Mitch let Ruben come over and help Jeannine up. By the time she limped in the door, Mitch was sitting next to Dawa, who was on the sofa, straight-backed, and dry-eyed. She was just sitting there, running her hand over her big old swollen middle, and humming. Mitch had his arm over her shoulders. "I know, girl," he said almost kissing her with his words, "I know."

No one spoke for the next few minutes. Then Dawa stood up, "I guess it's time to go. You folks go ahead, I think I'll walk." She looked at Ruben crossly, and raised her voice slightly, "By myself."

Ruben started to respond, and then thought better of it, and simply walked towards the door. Mitch leaned over and kissed Dawa on the cheek. "See you in a few. Stay strong."

Dawa snorted, "As if I have a choice." She held back the tears that were on the edge of her lashes. Jeannine came close and wrapped her arms around her friend, "You okay?"

Dawa shook her head, "I'll see you at M'dear's, okay? I just need to be myself for a few minutes."

Dawa waited until the others left, and then walked around the flat as if she was looking for something. After awhile she realized she could stall no longer, so she walked out the door and down the stairs. At the bottom of the stairs stood Victoria. She looked as if she was getting ready to walk up the front stairs towards Dawa's door. Victoria's lips were moving, but no words were coming out. The sounds seemed trapped in her little bird beak. Dawa didn't seem to see Victoria. Dawa was looking straight ahead, and didn't change her pace a bit as she edged past the frail older woman. As Dawa walked down the block, easy and steady, Victoria trailed just at her heels. Then after two more blocks, Dawa picked up her pace, and was moving almost in a trot, and Victoria was moving two steps in back of her, shadowing the woman. But as soon as Dawa reached the corner where her mother's house was, Victoria stopped up short. She called out Dawa's name, but her voice came out in a rasp, and Dawa did not hear. As Dawa took a deep breath and climbed the short flight of stairs to her mother's house, Victoria sped up and again tried to get the woman to turn around. She waved her arms and opened her mouth, trying to speak some words of comfort. She was still standing there, arms outstretched and lips slightly open, as Dawa opened the door and stepped inside.

11. Crossroads

Soon as Victoria sees Dawa is safely inside, she turns and starts walking towards downtown. I figured she was going to the church down the way, to stand in line for lunch. I let her clip-clop down a couple of blocks before I get ready to ask her why she was following Dawa.

"That was the first time I witnessed, and knew the relations. I cannot ignore the fact that that young woman lives in my building. I saw her brother pass, and I need to tell her what happened."

Well, of course I asked her how come she was moving her lips, but no words came out. I mean she certainly has no problem letting me hear her. Victoria stopped in her tracks and starts waving her arms and yelling at me. She had a small white handbag on a short strap, and it was swinging in my direction like some kind of a weapon. Meanwhile she is as loud as can be. She didn't seem to even notice these three young men, eyeing her, and getting closer and closer.

"You old crazy haint. Of course words were coming out. That young woman was just so upset she couldn't hear me. I declare one day you're calling me crazy, and the next you are accusing me of not talking, when I know full well I am speaking perfectly clearly. You are getting to be too much. If you don't have something sensible to say, why don't you just be still and let me take care of my business? I do not need you to be here speaking nothing but ignorance."

Well, right then, I tell her I do have something to say, and warn her of these three young boys coming closer and closer. They couldn't a been more than thirteen or fourteen years old. This was a time boys their age should have been trying to climb that mountain takes a boy into being a man. I could tell by the way they were swaggering, that sure as not, some of them would have died and not made it back to the village with their age mates, because they wouldn't had the sense to turn their back on death, or make the leap across the river of fears into knowing. But these boys didn't seem to have anyone telling them how to make the journey. It was like they were bored, or confused, or something. Full of hot air and spit, that's what they were. It was clear that Victoria wasn't the type to have anything of value to take, only her life. And seemed like I was the only one who took an interest in that. But these boys were coming to her like some bees coming to take nectar from a field of poppies. Before I finished telling her to get moving, they were circling around her, taunting her, and not letting her move down the street. The short one with his baggy pants about dragging on the ground spoke out, "Willie, she's just a crazy old white lady. Leave her be. She smells, too, just like old mothballs. Come on, let's go shoot some hoops."

"Naw, this is on a bet, and I'm winning this one. See, Raymond, she's colored. Just like Matt's Aunt Sandra. Only Matt's aunt knows she's black. Look." Well, this Willie boy sticks his hand up and starts trying to wipe off Victoria's makeup, while the other two boys just crowd close and keep her from moving.

"Maybe she's a ghost, Willie. I wouldn't touch her."

"She ain't no ghost, she's just a crazy old..."

Just then Victoria starts screeching and flapping her arms, like some kind of sea gull, like she was trying to take off. Well, of course, while they boys were crowding around, everybody on the street just walked by, hardly giving her or them a glance. But when the woman began her banshee yell, folks on the street seemed to run past trying not to see. The boys seemed like they were frozen too, as I cut through them and tried to shoo them away, but they couldn't tell I was there, so only one even backed up at my screams.

Well, you'd a thought one of those folks in the cars

driving by would have stopped and tried to help, but no one did until Sketch showed up. There he was, still in the same clothes from the night before, dried blood on his shirt, eyes all swollen, and tear tracks running over his cheeks. Here comes that boy towards Victoria. She just kept waving her arms, and blind-sided Jamal while he pushed back the tall one who had been touching her face. He tried to calm her down and catch her flying arms, but she just kept screeching and flailing her arms, and speaking in some kind of made-up language. Jamal got all scratched up, and the two of them fell to the sidewalk. All of the time, Jamal was talking to her, "It's okay. I don't want to hurt you. It's okay. Just calm down, no one is going to hurt you. Please, lady, calm down."

Now the other boys they backed up, but they were just watching Victoria and Jamal like it was the Saturday matinee at the movies. I realized that Victoria was going to keep carrying on until those boys were gone. I yell at them to get the hell out of here. But none of them could hear me except Jamal. He yelled out, "Yeah, get the hell away from here." Then the one they called Willie motioned to the other two, talking out the side of his mouth saying that it was "probably time to move on since the rollers are coming."

No sooner did these boys take off around the corner than the police walked on up. Victoria had just stopped yelling, and Jamal was helping her up off of the ground. The police caught Jamal by the arm and twisted his arm around his back, at the same time asking Victoria if the boy was bothering her. Victoria suddenly became stiff as a statue. She stood up, all fragile and stiff like one of those wine glasses she keeps in the cabinet and never uses. Then she turned her back on the policemen and Jamal. Talk about quiet. Nobody said a word. I could see her trembling as the police came closer.

Well, that Jamal, he didn't miss a beat. He told them that she was his aunt, and that she had just had a little fit, and that he was taking her home. I was pretty sure that she didn't want to go anywhere with him. And to tell you the truth, I was pretty sure that Jamal didn't want to go anywhere with her either. She had scratched up his face during her screaming, and I could see a trickle of blood coming out of one of the scratches, it ran from the corner of his eye all the way across his right cheek. But just then she started crying. Not making any noise but just crying. "They took my shield," she whispered. "I can't get home now, everybody will see me. I can't get home." Then she looks at Jamal, "Please see me home." The policeman dropped Jamal's arm and stood back.

Jamal was looking at her real hard. He could see her skin peeking out from underneath the white pancake makeup. It was a kind of yellow brown. And her white stockings were torn up and her hat had fallen off. Jamal just took her by her elbow and led her down the street, "Come on, I'll get you home. Won't nobody mess with you. If they try, I got plenty to give them today, a whole lot to pile on their behind."

Now, I don't remember the last time I saw anybody actually touch Victoria. I mean folks don't hardly see her, so you know they won't touch her. But here was this boy just walking with her, holding her real light, like she was some kind of glass that could break. The officers, they just looked at each other and shrugged. Then they went walking on down the street like nothing had happened.

When we got to her front door, Victoria reached up and put her hand on Jamal's face. Yes, she did! Her hand was gloved and all, but still she touched him. I swear I could of fallen out. Victoria knew it too, "Don't say a word," she fussed at me. So I didn't, and neither did Jamal. I think he thought she was talking to him. Then, while her hand was on the boy's cheek, she says, "I'm sorry, dear, I didn't mean to hurt you. Come on in and let me clean up your scratches."

I could tell Jamal didn't want to go inside. But he looked tired, too, like he wasn't sure what to do. I was betting he hadn't slept since he saw his Daddy pass, just ran. I was betting that he hadn't eaten either.

Well, right as I was adding up the situation, which kept coming up odd, Victoria straightened up real proud like and said, "Dear me. Of course you can't come into a stranger's house. Miss Victoria Cheevers, dear. I know your aunt lives upstairs. We've met."

"Jamal Everman, but folks call me Sketch."

"I'll call you Jamal. That is your given name. Please do come in, young man."

And in he went, just as docile as you please, and, as instructed, sat on the white sofa. Victoria went into the bathroom and got a washcloth and some soap; then she went over to the sink and filled a bowl with water and brought it to the boy. She sat right next to him and gently as could be washed off the blood, just dabbing it away like he was a baby. While she was in the bathroom she had powdered her face back, but she still hadn't taken off her gloves. "I was so sorry to see what happened to your father. You couldn't tell until he was dying, but when the bullets opened him up, child, it showed. He was just full of the light. It just poured out of him like a river. You have it too. But it shows in you, without you being opened up. In your eyes and your fingers. You got that dark brown color, kind of hides it. But I can see. I can see."

"I happen to like my color. Why do you paint yourself so? I can tell you're really black. Why do you hide it?"

"Why, I'm not hiding the color, child! I'm showing the light."

"Where'd you get that idea?" Jamal asked. Now I could hear the sarcasm in his voice coming through loud and clear. But Victoria, it's like she was just having someone to tea in her parlor, and having a nice little chat.

"Well, I don't really know when it first came to me. I suppose I was looking in the mirror, which means I was on my way out the door to somewhere. I am not one to waste hours upon hours in the mirror. But I do make sure that I am presentable. That is to say, I think before I go out my front door. I take the time to think about what people will see, and I think about the types of things they think about. I think what I will allow them to think about me, and what I will not allow. And I do my thinking in front of the mirror. Pressing back those strands of hair that insist on curling out across my face, smoothing a thin powder over my cheeks and neck, adjusting my collar and making sure that each button is buttoned properly. When I am seen, I want people to get the correct impression.

"It is not that I want to be seen. I am most comfortable when politely ignored. To tell you truth, I have never found that people in general offered me very much. But, if they insist on seeing me, they will see me properly. I carry that in my walk, in the way my head rests on top of my neck, high above my shoulders, and in the way my back holds straight, even though carrying a full load of years. I know I'm somebody. It is in my walk, in and how I've always walked, even before I had gotten as good at blending in, as good at being unseen.

"I am almost never seen. Sometimes I bet they see a bustle of passing white. Rarer still, I catch someone who sees me as a woman, and then again rarer than that, someone might see me as a colored woman if I move too slow. Mostly, only my own see down to the color. Ones like you, that have their own light. Of course, just like you, they don't always understand that I have not tried to stop being colored. They think, because of my praises in white, that I feel being a Negro is a disservice. But like I said, only a few people ever see me anyway. I don't get bumped into.

"It took me years to figure out how to make them stop seeing me. Someone might be walking down the street when they get a flash of me, my dress, my walk, my cape pulling behind me, and then, just as fast as they start to really look, I'm gone from their eyesight and they just turn their attention to someone else. If nobody sees you, you just don't get hurt.

Of course, you have to look after yourself. But then I have always done that, looked after myself.

"You know, there are thousands of shades of white. White is not just some blanket like summer clouds or cotton tufts or bleach. I know how to really see all the whites. They say that there is this white bright light when you die, and on the other side of that light you will find God—if you have lived correctly, of course. There is no light for the wicked, but then even the dumb ones know that. Of course, since that day when I began to see, I have gotten less sure about what makes someone wicked."

I thought that by then Jamal would have been tired of Victoria's crazy rambling. But instead of backing out the door, he asked her real polite if she would mind if he had a glass of water. Victoria almost jumped off of the sofa. I hadn't seen her move that fast and smooth in years. "Oh my, I am sorry to be so rude. I've been going on so. I have some cookies and some tea you can have."

Well, I was sure those cookies must have been stale. They were in a box that Victoria's niece had given her Christmas time. But the box hadn't been opened, so who knows? Victoria said she was saving it for tea, as if she ever had company for tea, tea or anything else. I was her only company, and I don't eat. Well, wouldn't you know it, teatime finally came.

Jamal got up and walked into the kitchen with Victoria, "How long have you been like this, Mrs. Cheevers?"

"Miss Cheevers, Jamal. Miss. Well, it was so long ago I have about forgotten how I lived before then. There was that day when I discovered how to make who I was show and not show at the same time. That was the day I learned how to pass up most trouble, and keep things light, keep things bright. The solution was in the white.

"I started with just the thinnest coat of foundation and a little face powder. It kept my perspiration to a minimum and made me all one smooth tone. My real color, just a breath deeper than buttermilk. I stopped wearing colors that day, except for the brocades, that's a creamy white over a harsher white, or sometimes I get a sweater with the little pearl beadwork near the collar, sometimes a rose blossom or a leaf, but always in a shimmering white. The shoes were always white, even my winter boots. And my stockings were always white, too. They don't last as long as they used to."

Now I'm always suggesting to Victoria that she might as well go out with her legs bare since they are always covered with a skirt anyway, and on top of that nobody can see them anyway. But she doesn't hear me.

"I have to wear stockings. I mean I could not wear slacks. I was brought up to wear dresses and that's what I wear. Now some women work some kinds of labor and they have to wear pants and I can understand that and I do not fault them one bit. But I have never been one of those women. I wear dresses, all days, all nights, always white, all different whites, but always white.

"Of course, I cover my hair. I did not stop wearing it out that day. It took a few years to realize that the oiling and brushing wasn't enough. I mean my hair was already somewhat light. Now though, I wear a scarf tied under my chin alone or up under my hat, if I have a hat. I like the round ones best, white again, always white. My hats are felt, mostly. That's what I can always find in the shades I need.

"I don't accept what some people would call a white. You'd be surprised how many people can't see what is, and what isn't, truly white. They don't use their eyes. They call a beige, or a banana, white. Now, when I go out, I am all white. I put on plenty of foundation. I do all of my neck into the hairline, and my hands and wrists. Oh, I know with the sleeves and gloves the hands never hardly show, but every once in a while a glove gets soiled with something wet, and you don't have another one just there, and you must take it off, and then the hands are just sticking out there, bare, for anyone to see, so I just rub on that cream base and powder them up too."

Victoria stopped her chatter and looked at Jamal, trying to see if he had understood her. I was pretty sure he understood that the woman was one fruitcake, but the boy surprised me again. Instead of mouthing off, like I'd seen him do to the police, and folks chasing him away from their walls, and even his father, he spoke to her real thoughtful like. "Well, I never have taken to too much that's white myself. And as for white, Mrs. Cheevers, no disrespect, but black is the one that is full of all kinds of colors. You look at some oil on the ground, when the light touches it, suddenly it's a rainbow. You look at obsidian, put it up to the sun, when the light touches it, you've got every color you can imagine, and some you can't. I try to mix colors to get all the colors you can see in the light. But some colors they just can't be mixed."

Victoria just smiled. By then she had the tea and the cookies ready. Jamal must have been real hungry, because he filled that cup of tea with all kinds of sugar, and ate the whole plateful of cookies. I don't think he even noticed that although Victoria poured herself a cup of tea, she never touched it, and she never reached for a cookie. Jamal just ate, quiet as can be—then, like he'd been waiting to ask, just saving it up, he said,

"My father was in green when he died. Bright green and some faded blue jeans. He didn't have any kind of white on him."

"I didn't say he was dressed in white, Jamal. I said he was full of light, streaming from inside of him. I saw the light coming out when he was shot."

"Well, if you saw my father murdered, you saw who did it, right? I mean maybe we could walk the streets some time, and you could point out the man, or the car, or something."

"They weren't going for him, child. Only the light pulled the bullets towards him."

"He froze, Mrs. Cheevers. He should have dropped, but he froze."

"Is that right?" Victoria said and then stood up and walked to the door. "Well, you'll have to be going now. Thank you."

"But, Mrs. Cheevers! I want to know what they looked like. The ones who shot him?"

"I witness the dying, boy, not the living. I can tell you about your father's passing, but you were there, so you know. I saw you trying to fill him back up with the light. You were pouring it in him. For a while I thought you might bring him back, he had so much of the light. But there were just too many holes. The more light you put in one place, the more poured out another. I saw you and your father, boy. That's what was important. In any case, I don't believe I'll be going out too much more."

Jamal stood at the door. "Maybe I could come back and check on you. I mean, if you want, I'll come back. You know, help out if you need something, or maybe want to go out and not worry. And maybe you'll remember something else about last night." And then Jamal's voice got all quiet and stuck up inside him as he muttered, "And maybe not."

Victoria ignored his mumbles, "Why, thank you, Jamal Everman, but I think we'll be fine."

"We'll? Who else..."

"Thank you again, Jamal Everman. We won't be seeing you again until the service. Perhaps you can ask your aunt to put a notice under our door. We'd like to pay our respects. After that, perhaps you can come and have some tea. We'll see."

Then Victoria opened the door and the sunlight came in full force. I could tell that Jamal could barely see her. She'd become just a wavy post of white, without arms, or eyes, or anything. He gave a shudder and then walked out the door. Victoria shut the door and then said to me, "Not a word. You hear me, not a word. You just leave me be." And then she turned on her heels and went into the bathroom.

I heard her running a bath. As the water ran, I saw her go into her bedroom and take out a long white nightgown and a fresh set of underwear. That woman actually sleeps in underclothes. I never would have survived having to wear all that clothing on me. Seems like the weight of all that cloth, and all those bands and buttons that pinch and squeeze, would smother the spirit in a body. But that's Victoria. Well, I saw she was in for the evening, so I just slipped under the door and went outside. I didn't want to be bothered with Victoria any more than she wanted to be bothered with me.

12. Funeral

the bones, white, are fed
to river, mountain, earth
laid underneath a tree,
the remains shaken to the wind
forgotten in time.

women are not allowed near the body.
we weep, moan, pull the spirit back.
it must fly through time,
meeting itself at the rainbow's edge.

it is black
it knows no color
it rides a melody
a long clear note
blown from a smoke-filled saxophone.

music to forever
it becomes
bird, star, tree.

they do not allow us near,
women moan, cry too loud
weep, remember too well.
only we can still the wind.

In the next few days, Dawa took care of all of the arrangements. She knew that Ranger had not wanted his body on view. He had told her many times that when he died, he wanted to be quietly cremated. And he wanted his ashes to be disregarded. "Come on, Sister, do you really think they're going to give you my ashes? Girl, it could be some redneck from a backwater swamp who still doesn't believe that Yankees won the Civil War. I tell you they just put a bunch of people in that oven and then fill jars with them. When I'm dead, I just want to be burnt up. Have a party with lots of food and plenty of liquor and let it go. Let me go."

When Lucille insisted on a full funeral service, Dawa fought and fought. Finally Ruben convinced her that the wishes of the living counted as much as those of the dead. So in a compromise it was agreed that there would be a service, and afterwards the body would be cremated. In another compromise Dawa agreed that she would get the ashes for Lucille, and would see that they were buried in a forest somewhere. Every time Dawa had to bend her will, her mouth filled with bile, and her throat filled with tears she refused to shed. By the time the day of the service came, she was a small hurricane moving through the city.

When Dawa climbed out of the small car, shut the door, and began walking towards the funeral home, she had no kind words for anyone. She started walking down the street without waiting for Ruben to catch up. Ruben reached in the back of the car and lifted out two large flower arrangements. He caught up to her and touched her elbow, but as far as Dawa was concerned he could have been on the moon. Dawa stayed just a few steps in front of Ruben. Dawa was still angry and had no words to share with her husband.

When Dawa entered the foyer, she went to a table at the

left of the sanctuary door and moved aside the funeral programs. Then she opened up her large handbag and pulled out a handful of pictures. There was Ranger playing with the family dog Griff, holding a stick high in the air as Griff leapt up to claim it. There was Ranger caught mid-dive going into Hamilton Pool, and Ranger running track on his high-school team. There was Ranger going to his senior prom with Janice, and Ranger with Jamal on his shoulders. The most recent picture of Ranger has been taken by Ruben, at the family reunion two years before. Ranger's face was long and gaunt. His eyes were sunk back in his head and brimming with tears, and his lips cracked open as if caught mid-sentence, or mid-prayer, as he squatted next to Jamal's half-sister, nine-year-old, fingers-in-mouth, neatly braided Evie. Dawa laid the photographs out in a circle and then put a banner across the wall. "*Elliott Everman, Junior—Thirty-seven years of living easy and living hard. We love you, Ranger.*"

She had spent hours the night before lettering the banner with various stencils. She had started with "*Elliott 'Ranger' Everman, Junior—Thirty years of living as a man. We love you.*" She figured that you couldn't really count the last seven that he spent slave to cocaine in all its incarnations, powder, liquid, and finally as pebbles in a long glass pipe. Ruben convinced her that she should tone it down if she wanted to be welcomed by her family at the funeral. "Like I want to go anyway," Dawa had spit out and returned to her careful calligraphy, rephrasing her thought. This time she wrote, "*Elliott Everman, Junior—Thirty years of living, and seven years of dying. We loved you the best we could, Ranger.*" Ruben shook his head in disgust. "Dawa, this is no time for a campaign. You are supposed to be honoring the dead." When Ruben reached for the paper the second time, Dawa took a swing at his jaw. Ruben ducked and just got grazed. He was sure that the baby she was carrying would definitely come out mean-tempered because of the anger that had flowed like hot lava from Dawa every time she opened her mouth.

"I am acknowledging the truth of his life, Ruben." Finally she came up with her compromise. Not as direct as she would have liked it, but sedate enough not to aggravate too many in the family. As she finished arranging the photographs, she found her brother Newcomb at her elbow. "Hey, Sis, I'd say the hard years about ate up the years of living easy. But you got it about right." Dawa smiled. She had known Newcomb would understand.

"Dawa, I got these out of the family album from mama's living room last night. Didn't dare ask her for them. She looked at it till she fell asleep. I slipped them out, but, girl, you'd better get these back on their pages today."

Newcomb had brought pictures of the four children. The annual Easter picture, year after growing year. Ranger and Newcomb were always in suits, with ties pinching their Adam's apples, and shoes that sparkled even in black and white. Ranger always towered over the other three children. Elise was properly formal with her wide-skirted dresses and perfectly curled hair. Dawa was invariably looking the wrong way, cracking a silly grin, or smoothing down a wayward lock of hair. The prize picture Newcomb brought was the one with Ranger and his mother. There she was, holding her one-year-old baby boy, who was reaching up and putting his fingers in his mother's mouth. She was obviously trying to get him to turn around and pose for the camera, but was laughing as he smiled and reached for the kisses that he knew were always forthcoming from Lucille. The last picture was Elliott Senior, and Elliott Junior, playing baseball. Elliott Senior was getting ready to pitch, and Elliott Junior was standing, legs spread too far apart, teeth biting into his top lip, eyes squinted. The father was grinning broadly, and the son was just beginning to swing. Dawa ran her fingers over the photos. "Who would have known?" she whispered. "Who could have seen it back then, back when?"

Dawa turned from the table and entered the chapel. She walked down the center aisle slowly. Her older sister, Elise, sat stiff and dry-eyed near the back of the room, and the twins sat between their uncle and grandmother. Opposite Elise, looking frayed and shrunken, was Hoodoo. Hoodoo and Ranger had run together since they were in high school. They had met as teenagers, and returned as men with more scars inside than out. Hoodoo had left one of his legs near the Mekong Delta. Ranger had left all of his faith in the same spot. Still, when they came back, they broke the odds and remained friends. Where one went, the other went, even if it meant going to hell and not coming back.

Dawa saw Jeannine and Mitch. Evie was leaning up against her mother, her eyes, opened wide as saucers, refusing to let herself cry. Michael was sitting next to Mitch as tall as he could. He kept glancing back, hoping his brother was going to come in. Dawa saw her uncle and aunt and a few old friends of the family, quietly talking to each other, a tape of Sly and the Family Stone playing in the background. Dawa smiled. She and Mitch had worked to put the tape together. She could almost see Ranger's long lanky body poking the corners of the room as he rocked and dipped to "Every Day People," and laughed as she heard Elise hiss out, "How inappropriate! This is supposed to be a funeral." Dawa leant over to her sister and sang softly, "There is the black one, that can't accept the white one, that doesn't like the yellow one. Different strokes..." Elise softly pushed Dawa's head away. It was then that Dawa realized that she hadn't seen Jamal. She stood up and slowly took her eyes across the room. That was when she saw Victoria tucked in a corner. But Ranger's son was nowhere to be found. All in all, the room was mostly empty. Gaps in the pews were held together by an unerring silence.

An usher put a program in Dawa's hand, and she sank into a seat next to her mother, who accepted her kisses but did not look at Dawa. Tape music changed to "Mary Don't You Weep," sung by Aretha Franklin. It, too, was one of Ranger's favorites. When it ended, Dawa got up and in a dry, flat voice read the short biography that was printed in the program, "Elliott Lincoln, Junior was a graduate of Polytechnic High School. A member of the city's All-Star Little League Baseball team, Elliott dreamed of becoming a professional. At nineteen he was drafted and sent to Vietnam where he earned a bronze medal. Those who knew Elliott knew that he was always quick with a smile and ready to pitch in and help a friend. He was also dangerous on the dance floor. Elliott returned home after being wounded in combat. He trained in carpentry and worked in construction on and off until his death. He is survived by his son, Jamal; his sisters, Elise, and Dawa; his brother, Newcomb; his mother, Lucille; and a host of aunts, uncles, nephews, nieces, and cousins."

When she finished, Dawa looked at the small assembly. She was supposed to sit down, but she didn't. She stood looking at the program in her hand. Turning it over as if there was supposed to be something more there. There wasn't, so she decided to add the missing parts, "Ranger, Ranger taught me so much when I was a little girl. He always told me to speak up—not that I needed being told." The people in the room quietly laughed, glad for a moment to lift the weight of the air that was stifling them. If there was one person who always would speak their mind, asked or not, it was certainly Dawa. "You know Ranger, Elliott Junior, didn't want all of this." She lifted her arms, indicating the coffin and then the pews. "He wanted us to just let him go. But since we're here, I'm not going to let him be known as just some kind of a shadow. He was so much more than these few words, more than a Vietnam veteran. It was Vietnam that taught him to be proud of being black. I mean that's where he found out exactly where Africa was, and figured out why he and so many of his buddies filled the front lines.

"And he was more than a construction worker. A whole lot of people around here, with only little bits of money, can look at the wall Ranger repaired, or the closet he built for them, or the garage he fixed for little more than a meal and a bed for the night. Even when he didn't have his own home, he helped other people build theirs. And he isn't just survived by Sketch, I mean Jamal. He was a father to Jamal as much as he could be..." People shifted around looking for the sixteen-year-old boy, the pride of his father. "Sketch, Jamal, is going to survive because Ranger finally showed him the strength to climb out of his hole.

"He finally almost came back to the man I knew, but he just wasn't strong enough. There were some years I could barely look at my brother. I didn't want to see his skeleton body and watery eyes reaching out to me for a couple of dollars, or a night on my couch. But I know this, I always loved my brother. And I'm sorry he didn't make it all the way out of that hole he dug for himself. And I am so mad..."

Tears were brimming in her eyes as Ruben leapt up to pull her from the podium before she said any more. She didn't resist him. The pastor of Lucille's church got up to speak. He didn't really know Ranger, so he spoke instead about Lucille, about the family that Ranger came from, about the idea of eternal peace and a final release from the pain he had been living in. As he began to talk about the devil that was stalking the streets, the devil that had taken a hold of Elliott Junior's soul and was pulling him down to a fate he could not escape, Lucille stood up and stopped his sermon,

"I have something to say."

Everyone shuffled and looked toward the dark, cloaked woman, thin, not frail, gray biting at the brown of her skin. She stood smelling like the parlor, too thick with gladiolus and lilies. She looked all around the room. Her voice came out so clear it was like a chiming bell.

"Now, you all have spoken and sang, but you haven't talked about nothing. So, I have something to say and I'll just say it now."

Newcomb sank lower in his hard smooth seat,

"Damn, M'dear"

Dawa grabbed at her mother's arm. "M'dear, Mama."

The woman standing between them hadn't been young in a very long time, and couldn't really be called old; she shook off her daughter's hand as if it was a troublesome fly. She looked at Dawa and Newcomb to let them know that they had been heard and considered. Then she walked to the front of the hall, indicating to the pastor that he needed to move away from the pulpit. Her voice was sure and came out like burning fire tongs carefully holding red hot shards of coal.

"I have something to say right here and right now, and you will allow me to say it. I want you all to hear me, and damn it I want God to hear me too."

Under her breath, Elise asked Jesus to intervene, as she fanned herself hard and nervously.

"What's a matter, Elise?" the woman turned to her sister. "You so tied up in that Bible that you always are quoting, that you haven't noticed that God always seems to make it for the dying even if he don't always be on time for the living? Just like you folks, huh?"

Whispers screeched against the walls. She walked slowly, straight-backed and gentle across the length of the pews, seeking out their eyes one by one, daring them to turn aside or shush her. She moved to the coffin, pulled back the black gauze lying over her son, and shed her first tear since the night of his death. Then 'Lil Bit, Tiny Thing, a Inch and a Half of Feather, swelled in size and began to sob. First it was barely audible, but in a few moments it became a soft wail, with no breaks or breaths, filling the corners of the hall.

Dawa moved forward quickly, "Mama."

Her mother looked up, impatiently waving the daughter back to her seat.

"Be still, child. Hush." Then she lifted herself, wet-faced and grim, and shifted to the altar.

"My child is dead. YOU HEAR ME? My first born is," and she held the word rolling it around her tongue, knowing that to say it one more time was to finally believe it, "dead, gone forever, and he wasn't but thirty-seven, but he's dead. Ain't that something, all those dreams gone forever?"

The congregation sat back, waiting for her public mourning to end. Her children wished it had happened later, at home, where it was more easily hidden. The pastor was disturbed because he was cut off in what promised to be one of his better services; and her friends were suddenly flea-bitten and cramping with loose bowels, hoping that her words would be brief, understandable, but indefinite, leaving them with no responsibility besides the understanding, "Un huh, I hear you, Lucy."

Lucille, clear-voiced, continued, "I held him in my arms to the last. He looked at me with those lying I-ain't-loved-no-woman-like-I-love-you eyes, and he touched my face. You know what he told me that last night he slept at home? He said he was broken, and just wasn't sure he was going to make it all the way back. He asked me to love him and keep him warm like I always did, and don't cry. I was cradling him in my arms, and he was just dry sobbing, asking me to forgive him for not being so strong, for not being the son he was supposed to be. He was wearing the shirt I gave him for his birthday, just a few days before. He thought I forgot to get him anything, because I leave it be so much. But this year, this year, I believed he was going to make it back to being a man. This was the year he was going to stay clean.

"I know he was doing better, sometimes when he came by the house, he looked like he was starting to get the shine back in his eyes. He knew he had to get Jamal into manhood. I told him to stop that foolishness. He was plenty strong, I told him. He'd been clean for four months pressed together, and I knew he could do it another four, and then another, and it would be a year. And I told him so until he believed me. I told him so until he was telling it back to me. "You right, Mama," that's what he said, all full of pride again. "Yeah, you will see. I'm gonna do better by my son. Better for you."

He was almost back, I know it. He was coming all the way back to being the man he really was.

"Funny, when he was a baby, we'd always laugh about how it seemed like he was a man since he could walk. You know when they called me to the hospital last week and there he was all tied to all those machines. He had tubes up his nose and going into his veins and monitors just beeping and flashing, and there he was. He seemed so short, and he was so thin, so thin. Of course Elliott was always on the bony side, but that sickness it took all his flesh, it took everything, even the sparkle in his eye. And I didn't think nothing would ever take that.

"I went in that room, and I was going to bring my child back. You hear me? He was coming back. So I just sat down on that bed, and slipped under all those wires, till I could cradle him in my arms, and just sing to him, like I did when he was full of fever and swollen with the mumps. Elliott was warm, and he smelt like these flowers, and the grease from the street, and smoke, and he was so small. I swear, I heard him moan. Oh, those doctors can talk about their comas and brain-dead all you want, but I heard him. I heard him gasp when I picked up his head. He moaned, and I rocked him like he wasn't but a year old, and sang to him. I sang to him till Elise had them to turn off that breathing machine. It had been so loud in the room, with that wheezing and blowing. But when they turned off the machine, it got so quiet and still, and I just sang some more. He kept breathing, you know. They said he would die right off, but he kept breathing another hour. I just held on and sang, and I tried hard as I knew how; I tried to pull my baby back. I held him till he didn't breathe no more, till he was limp and folded over, till he fell out of my arms.

"My child, mine. I held him, he moved first inside me. I taught him to say mama, and black, and free. I told him he wasn't born to be a servant to white folks. I gave him God, and told him to believe. I told him about family, how they was his guns and his barricades, and how his neighbors was his crutches when he got weak. I told him to love, to trust, to be a man, and he believed me. He believed me! He always, whatever he might have done, he always believed. *Mama*, he'd say, *mama, I love you because you don't never tell me wrong*. And I guess, I never did until then."

She paused, returned to his casket, grazed her eyes over the length of his body, brushed her gloved fingertips across his face, "This isn't my son! This child here isn't my son! Look at how small he is. My son was tall, just like his daddy. The sun always shined over his left shoulder when he walked. He'd pick weeds for me, and call them flowers, and that's what they'd be, the most beautiful flowers in the whole city. *For my African queen*, he'd say, and bow real deep like I was born of royalty, and I'd bow my head like any queen would do when given such a special gift, and then we would bend over laughing."

She smiled, cushioned for a moment with remembrances.

"He was browner than this child. This one is kinda gray and flat, but my boy, my boy was a deep brown like yam-planting earth, and his head scraped every ceiling it was under, and he laughed so pure and long, you'd forget your troubles inside his joking. This child here is shriveled, and weak, and stiff. This child looks like he never knew no laughter, or peace neither, not even now. But my boy—why, my boy was calm and deep like the midnight sky. All the ladies loved that about him, how he would move from quiet and deep, to lightning laughter, as easily as you step off a curb. Yes, isn't no lady been wooed till my boy winks in her direction. No folks, no, this here just isn't my boy."

She stiffened as her son's image danced in front of her eyes, smiling again as tears began to stream from under her long lashes, but no sound of weeping could be heard. Her eyes began to grind into the assembly. They squirmed, straightened collars, readjusted crossed legs, fiddled at rings on swollen fingers, wiped away sweat. They waited.

Jeannine cried, caught in her own memories of his touch, his lips, their dreams. Once she was his woman. He had made her believe she could do anything, be anything. He had made her believe, as no one until then, not even her mother, had made her believe, that she was loved; that she had the right to expect everyone to honor and respect her, that she was special. But then he turned, he got further and further away. Everything he had made her feel about herself, he recanted. Every loving stroke he denied. He kept running into walls in his dreams, and he wouldn't, or couldn't, climb over them, or knock them down. So instead he knocked her down, and finally Jeannine took Jamal and moved out, and did not return. Jeannine had come to the funeral for Dawa and Jamal, and Jamal wasn't even there. But Jeannine did not tremble at the old woman's sermon; she knew she had tried to be there.

"The police say he was on his way to buy some of that dope, and got caught in a drive-by. Before he passed, he used to come around telling me how his head hurt, how it was full of so many ugly things he'd seen until they just wanted to explode all over the pavement. He said that little smoke made the headache go away. Said everything was clear and understandable, and the world wasn't moving too fast when he tasted that smoke. You know the feeling don't you, Billy? That's your name, ain't it?" Hoodoo looked towards the old woman, but didn't really see her. "How much did that last rock cost him? Was it ten or fifteen? You tell me, because here," she rushed back to her seat, pulled up a black clip-top leather bag, grabbed a twenty from its wallet, and threw it towards the man, "Here—will this cover the bill? Will it?" Her voice bled rage, and Billy, the boy's best friend, turned away from the woman who gave him bed and meals without question, from the time Elliott Junior had told her how he had saved his life in Vietnam, more than once. Hoodoo had even stolen from her, but she let him back in, saying she owed him a debt that could never be repaid. It was Ranger who finally chased Hoodoo from Lucille's doorstep. Mouth open, with no words in his brain or heart, Hoodoo turned away.

She found Hoodoo's eyes, "Where were you when he first started selling? You here, almost as gray as the boy in that coffin, nothing but skin and sweat hanging on your bones, where were you? Were you his best customer as well as his best friend? Who didn't stop the other? And when you got caught, when it was just a toehold instead of your whole body, how come you didn't come get me? Didn't I always nurse you when you were sick? Didn't you tell me we three could talk about anything. 'Hip Mama'—that's what you named me, said I was too cool. What's that mean, too cool? Too cool to stop my son from dying? Too cool to see you boys drifting further and further from me?"

Suddenly she let Hoodoo go, daring him to leave the room, wheeling with revolver tongue towards the pastor,

"And you with your pie in the sky; promising him the same tomorrows you promised his daddy when he wanted todays. *Get a job frying chicken*, you said, *at least it's a job. Why, when I was your age*. When you were his age you were already preaching, and living in a four-bedroom house we all helped pay for. When you were his age, you knew life could be real easy on a handful of hope for the congregation, and a plate full of change for the pastor. To tell the truth, you've never been his age. You've never taken chances, or seen any way other than turning cheek after cheek after cheek, calling it the Christian," she spat the word onto the floor—"the Christian way. Well, I sure hope he got his by and by, because if not, then that's just one more lie you are going to have to pay for on Judgement Day."

Her hand jutted from her side as she pulled her oldest daughter's eyes into her own, "And you, Elise."

Elise sat, head held high, shoulders back, long skirt covering her uncrossed legs, dry eyed and almost impatient.

"You, Miss Elise, when he wanted something he could touch, believe in again, you, the oldest, turned away, judging but not giving. Didn't I teach you no better? I know I said there was right and wrong, but not one right, lots of rights, lots of ways. You aren't a success because you made it on your own. You are a success because of all of us, everybody rooting you on through school, finding a dollar there, or giving up their room to sleep on the couch, so you have privacy and a place to study, just believing. Why didn't you believe in him like he believed in you? You took it all so for granted.

"Sam, Sam," she looked at the stout, sad man and shook her head slow and soft, "Sam, you promised his Daddy, you promised me, you promised him, you would be there. When he was trying to crawl out of all that mess, trying to do right. When he was finally really, really trying, that day when he came to tell you he didn't like hanging out, and couldn't you give him a job. You sent him to a friend of a friend, of someone you kinda knew, when what he needed was to be with someone who cared. Yeah, I know you told me you couldn't afford to take the risk. My, but you sure could afford to fill up this church with lovely flowers, and help me pay for the funeral, so he could go out like he should. You could afford that. Tell me how many more payments on your new Eldorado would it have been if you let him work with you? I know, I know, *It's a lot to ask, Lucille, a lot to ask.* I tell you now, like I told you then, sometimes friends ask a lot, and if it ain't impossible, why, real friends come through. That was your godchild. That means that was your child."

"And you, Mistuh Meanstuff," she turned to a dapper man, sitting in a tailored wool suit, with his hat held carefully across his lap. Although over fifty, he was the kind that wears their age in attitude more than wrinkles or gray. "Yeah, you Damone, you knew the streets better than you know the lines on your face. You and his daddy ran together, grew together, even did some time together, if I remember right—and I'm sure I do. So you, with the easy line, and pre-cise dictionary analyses of every situation, *Mr. If-I-don't-know-it-or-can't-*

find-it, it-ain't-there-to-know-or-be-found, why didn't you try to teach him what I couldn't know? Damone, when he got out a jail that first time, when it could still be stopped, or when you knew who he was running with and what it was going to mean, why didn't you talk to him? Why didn't you tell me? Couldn't you find time for one warning, one guiding word?"

"My son wasn't a crackhead. He wasn't a criminal. He wasn't a ruthless gang member. He wasn't a terrorist. He didn't rape women; he loved them. He was a king with no crown, with no land, with no people, with no family."

The tears began again, came like a river making her lips shine, brushing against her teeth. "Wasn't no white man killed my child, whitey didn't have a chance. And it wasn't no dope either. It was these streets, filled with all of you, and still all the way empty. I tried to protect him. I tried the best that I knew how. But, I couldn't do it alone. I couldn't do it by myself."

Her face became young as the river smoothed out her wrinkles. Her voice began to tremble,

"I thought we was a people, moving together, working together. I didn't mean to lie to my child. I thought you would be there. I didn't know. I didn't know. I didn't know."

She sank over the coffin. She kissed the youth on his eyes and lips. "I'm so sorry, I wish I knew better. I'm so sorry, baby, I did the best I could. God knows I loved you, and taught you the best I could." She had finished. She lay there, draped over the edge of the casket, crying softly.

The church was still, frozen, cold.

13. Endings

Dawa walked, by herself, to her mother's home after the funeral. When she reached it, she found Hoodoo sitting on the steps. He looked up at Dawa. "I'm sorry, Dawa. I wish I..." The man stopped mid-sentence and his eyes filled with tears. "We been through a lot, me and your brother. It might not look like it, but we never stopped trying to keep each other alive."

Dawa looked at Hoodoo sitting there, so very thin, skin dry and gray-edged. His eyes were slim, holding out the glint of sun in the sky and keeping others from looking too far in. She cut off his words, "Well, he was going to make it. I know he was. He was going to make it all the way free."

Hoodoo grabbed her hand and gave it a squeeze, "He already made it, Sister. He was getting strong again. He just didn't have enough time for all of you to see how far he came. He went too far to go back."

"You go back all the time."

Hoodoo sighed, "Naw. I never get loose. I just get it to ease its grip. But I'm never all the way clean. Ranger, he was through the door."

"Not far enough. Three hundred forty-four places you can buy beer in this city. Why would he go to that store? Plenty of places that were closer—come on, Hoodoo. Mama might want to believe that, but I'm just not going to..."

Hoodoo stood up and almost lost his balance. He held onto the banister to steady himself. Dawa reached out.

"I got it," Hoodoo snapped, and pulled himself up tall.

"Sometimes, Dawa, you need to go look at it, and tell it no. You got to be able to do it to her face. You know just have it there gleaming in your face, just reaching out and stoking that part of you that just writhes and yearns for it, and say no. No more."

"I'se free massa, I'se free." Dawa drawled out.

"Something like that." Hoodoo laughed back.

Dawa sneered, "Well, the way I heard the story, those that got away didn't look back. They just kept moving on."

Hoodoo probed Dawa's face. Looking for his words, reaching to make sense to her, trying to have the tongue that Ranger had, full of jokes and tales and answers. "Problem with us is that there is no north. We're going to meet up with those chains every day. We're going to smell it coming out of someone's house. We smell in their skin; we see the way they fidget at a stoplight and know. And we hear it steady talking in our ear, telling us. 'It's alright baby, you know you want me. Just a little bit. A little bit won't hurt.' Dawa, it's a chant inside of us, 'Work for me and I'll make you feel better. Work for me and I'll make everything better.' And you know it's a lie, but maybe, maybe this time it won't be. No, Dawa, you got to look her in the face and tell her no more. Say you can shake your butt in my face all you want, but no more. Yeah, Ranger did that that night. I know he did. He wasn't there to cop."

"Yeah, well, Hoodoo, I hope you're right. I really do. Not that it makes a difference. I mean if he had just not looked back, he might still be there. You know, *like Satchel said, don't look back, something might be gaining on you.* Come on in and have some food, Billy James. You know you need some. Mama was..."

Hoodoo cut her off mid-sentence, "I just came to tell you I'm sorry...and to tell you, he made it through. I know he did."

"And you, Hoodoo, what about you? You gonna 'make it through?'"

"Some of these folks out here with me, they're the only family I have." Hoodoo shook his head and walked to the sidewalk.

Dawa walked down to him. “Come on in; let me fix you a plate.”

Hoodoo smiled at her, “Last month, ’fore I got sick again, your brother took me out to that park in Oakland, that Tilden Park. The one with all the trails and everything. Got me up in all these trees, off the road. No stuff, no food, and my side aching. He took me up there, and started talking about smelling the green. Now far as I’m concerned you want to smell something green, you can stick your nose is some baby’s doodoo diaper. Smelling green. Well, he started talking about how different it smelled than the Nam. Started talking about the birds here, and the ones over there, how they sung differently. Y’know, he knew some of the names of the birds over there. Ain’t that some shit? Said he wanted to get back that feeling he used to have, where he wasn’t worrying about living or dying. He was just getting up, and taking the day as it came. Like if he had to kill somebody, he did it. And if he was going to get killed, well, that was real too. I was always having to pull his dumb butt out of the line of fire, warn him not to step there, because he just kind of took it like it came, and didn’t always pay attention like he should have. That was Ranger’s problem. He just didn’t pay attention like he should have. If I’d a been there, Dawa, I’d a pulled his green-smelling behind out of the fire one more time, just like he did me...just like he did me...” His voice tapered off and stopped. Eyes brimming with tears, Hoodoo turned and started walking, stiff-legged, to the corner without a word of goodbye.

Dawa climbed back up the stairs and went inside. Fewer than two dozen people stood and sat around the living room. Lucille was sitting in the armchair facing the fireplace. Dawa walked over and kissed her mother on the cheek. Lucille reached up and rubbed Dawa’s cheek without looking at her. Her gaze was captured by the drawing leaning against the mantelpiece in front of her. Ruben, Jeannine and Mitch, and Newcomb were standing next to the fireplace looking at the almost-finished picture of Ranger. There he sat, gaunt, but clear-eyed, leaning forward, legs spread, an elbow propped on each knee. His chin on top of his two-handed fist, and his mouth was partly open. The eyes were looking straight out, so that when you viewed the drawing, it seemed as though they were looking at you. The picture was two-thirds done. The bottom of one leg was barely sketched in, the top lip was only suggested, the face scar was not yet drawn in. Only the eyes were fully shadowed, with fine crisscrosses wedged at each outside corner. Sketch had colored in the pupils, a dark shiny brown, and filled in most of the shirt in a bright, thick green. Over the top, letters shaped in a banner flew across the paper, "FOR MY FATHER R.I.P." Shooting out from the letters were waving lines in yellow and gold, shimmering across the top of the page.

Dawa came close, "Where's Jamal?"

Mitch sneered, "Running the streets."

Dawa reared up, "Just because he isn't here..."

Jeannine cut in, "Dawa, let's go to the kitchen. Jamal will turn up. Lucille says the picture wasn't there when she left the house this morning, so he's around."

Mitch growled out, "Not where he's supposed to be."

"Who made you the judge and jury of where Jamal is supposed to be?" Dawa snapped out, relieved to finally have a pointed target for her anger.

Jeannine turned Dawa around and started pulling her out of the room. Dawa moved with her. It gave her a chance to avoid being a part of the inevitable "remember whens," or "he sure did like," or "I knew that man was going to..." Dawa didn't want to clutch him close one more time before she let him go.

Mrs. Bailey grabbed Dawa as she and Jeannine tried to pass,

"Your brother has gone to a more peaceful place."

"Well, now, that wouldn't be hard to do, would it, Mrs.

Bailey? Seems to me most places are more peaceful than here."

Mrs. Bailey drew in her breath. "I was just saying I don't think he is burning in hell fires... I know he had a relationship with Christ."

"And I'm just saying, he already got burnt up in hell. And thank you, yes, you are right. My brother has gone to a more peaceful place." Before she could get out her sarcastic "Praise be," Jeannine had steered her into the kitchen. As the door swung shut behind them, Dawa turned on Jeannine,

"Uh Jeannine, did I suddenly lose my ability to know when I want to leave a room, and when I want to stay in one?"

"Dawa, you know Mrs. Bailey has a weak-enough heart as it is, and you don't need to be raising her blood pressure. Besides she was trying to be nice."

"Please, she and my mother aren't even that close. She just came to cluck her tongue, pick up some gossip, and eat some food."

"Well, she brought a mess of the food that's here, so she needs to eat."

At that, Dawa changed the subject, "I think I'll stay with my mother for this next while."

Jeannine sat down at the kitchen table, "Girl, are you crazy? You are getting ready to have a baby. I think you'll stay with your husband."

"Jeannine, I think you'll get out of my business."

"Well, I tell you what, when we don't share no blood with our folks, and all the years we've known each other have disappeared, I'll get out of your business."

"Well, why don't you wait on an invitation to jump in then?"

"Got one right here." Jeannine put her hand over her heart, then she reached out her arms and pulled Dawa close and held her for a moment. "Saw you crying at the service. I thought you didn't cry in public. In fact, rumor has it you don't cry at all."

"You know damn well I cry. But I was dry-eyed at the service. That was Elise."

"So what now? I'm blind, dumb, and don't have any kinship rights?"

"Mama doesn't need to be alone."

"I thought Newcomb was staying with her."

"Yeah, but he won't do like Mama needs. Anyway she'll spend her whole time waiting on him."

"Maybe that's what she needs to do."

"She needs to take it easy."

Jeannine laughed, "Oh yeah, and having you and your about-to-burst-your-water-self over here is going to be real relaxing."

"Ruben is like a damned mother hen. I wish he'd just leave me alone. I mean when he needed to be waking me up and telling me something is wrong, he's being doofus. And now when he needs to let me be and find my own level, he's got a comment, or a criticism, or a something else, every other minute. When I'm supposed to be riding, when I'm supposed to be walking, how much sleep I haven't been getting, what I should or shouldn't be worrying about."

"Yeah, I see your point, Dawa. It's a damn drag having someone adore you."

"Hey, I don't have any problem with adoration, Sister-love. It's taking all those damn directions that's sending me up the wall. The last time I looked, I had a brain in my head."

"Yes, but were you using it?"

"Jeannine..."

Jeannine pulled her chair close to Dawa's and leaned over and put her arms around her again. Dawa held on to Jeannine as she whispered, "I'm just so afraid, Jeannine, for Jamal, for this baby, for Ruben, for us. It seems like everything is falling apart. I'm just so afraid, and I know if I show it, that'll be it.

If I show it for an instant, all the ghouls will take advantage and..."

Dawa began to hiccup, trying to hold back her tears. Her nose began to run, and the sobs were like sharp barbs cutting into her throat. Jeannine rubbed Dawa's back, whispering into her ear, "Go on and cry, baby. We're all afraid. You cover it up real good, just like Mitch. Both of you, all brag and strut, but soft as mush inside. Go on and cry. And then when you're done, pull yourself together, because you've got to help me find Jamal."

Dawa sat up and pulled in her sniffles. Jeannine pulled her back again. "No, baby, you finish crying first."

Just then Mrs. Bailey came in with an empty platter. She moved to the stove and refilled the platter with chicken, and went back out without saying a word. Ruben came in and started to move towards Dawa. Jeannine waved him away. He went back into the living room. The two women stayed there crying, talking, and crying some more, until deep into the night, until the last guest had left and Lucille had fallen asleep, sitting in the overstuffed chair, facing the unfinished drawing of her eldest son.

14. Markers

"You could have called. Folks are worried." Jackie shivered in the fog and pulled her sweater tight around her shoulders. She could feel the chill coming up through her thick socks, as she stood in the doorway. Sketch could see that Jackie's hair was being braided. One side bushed out while the other hung past her shoulder in long single braids. Sketch perched on the banister. He looked at her but didn't answer.

Sketch's aunt had called Jackie's house less than an hour earlier, "I'm sorry to bother you again, Jackie. I know his Mom already called, but I wanted to make sure you had my number, too." Dawa was the one who told her *why* he had to call. Jeannine had simply said that it was important, family business.

Jackie had just held the phone for a few minutes listening to Dawa matter-of-factly give out some details of her brother's death. "Does Sketch know?"

Dawa sighed, "Yes, the police say that he was there, that he saw it all. Jackie...," Dawa paused, "he didn't come to the funeral. I was sure he'd be there. He came by his grandmother's house, and left a picture, but no one saw him. Well, it's been three days since that and... If you see him, if you could just ask him to check in."

Jackie could hear the tremble in Dawa's voice. "Of course, I'll let him know, but you know, your nephew and me, we're not really kicking it anymore. I mean it's been months since he's done more than call, and anyway he's mostly staying in Frisco now, you know. So I mean..."

"Jackie," Dawa had an edge in her voice now. "If he comes by."

"I'm sorry, Dawa. Of course, if he calls or comes by I'll

make sure. I'll call you and his mom so you two know, and I'll try and get him to call, too, or go home. For sure. And I'm sorry about your brother. Sketch took me to meet him once. He was nice, real nice. Great jokes." There was a long silence. Both of them quietly remembered a moment, then Dawa voice broke across the phone line, "Yeah, he was one funny guy." She had sighed and hung up the phone.

Jackie looked at Sketch. His face showed salty lines of dried tears, his eyes small, squinting, red. His arms hung at his sides. His coat was unzipped and showed a blood-stained shirt. His mouth was open as if he was trying to speak, but no words were coming out. Jackie stepped closer to Sketch, but he backed away. She tried to smile as she pulled the sweater closed again, "Guess Indian summer is sure enough over now." Sketch did not respond.

Jackie moved close and put her hand on Sketch's face, "Jamalman, you coulda called. Your mom is worried, and your aunt just called."

"I'm calling now. I'm calling you," Sketch stood apart.

"Sketch, I know your..." Then she stopped herself. "I heard that your father was..."

"Can I stay here for a minute? I..." He stood trying to form the words in his mouth, needing to give a name to what he had seen the week before, how his father had felt light and airy in his arms, how he knew, before he even reached the hospital, that his father had just let go; how everything had changed and he didn't know how. All he knew was that his world, the world, his father...he could not find the words. He gulped back the air, holding his tears in his throat.

Jackie fit her arms around him, distantly, barely touching his back and sides, as if she was afraid to break something, him, herself. It never quite worked, boyfriend, girlfriend, lovers. But they kept coming back to each other, trying to have something that would work, and then Sketch would start to move apart, take some space, get some air. Jackie missed the talks they had that went for hours, and the silences, Sketch doing a piece on an alley wall and she writing in her journal, dreams, questions, days she didn't want to forget. Finally after too many break-ups, and since Sketch had decided to stay with his grandmother in San Francisco most of the time, Jackie started to date someone else. When Sketch had come by in early June, she wasn't available. He hadn't come back.

"You can stay here, for a minute, like you said. But you know we're not...I mean I'm not..."

Sketch pulled her closer, clung to her and began to sob, dry broken muffled yelps. "It'll be alright," she whispered into his ear, kissing his steamy face. They stood like that for a few minutes, until he stilled himself, but still he clung to her. Jackie felt the damp heat rising from his shirt, smelled the layers of sweat rising from his neck. She pulled away. "My mom is out. You can wait in my room. But you won't be able to leave until she does, in the morning. You know. But nobody'll bother you." She pointed to her head. "I gotta get..."

Just then a voice came breaking down the hall, a wave getting ready to break. "Hey Jack-Q-line. I got to get back to Hayward tonight. So you get your butt back here and let me finish..."

"Hold up, Bernie, I'll be in a couple."

"Go on. Wait in my room." Sketch didn't move. Jackie started to pull him inside. "Sketch, Bernie minds her own business. Don't trip. Come on."

Sketch couldn't move. He had spent the week running, stopping, catching his breath, running, sitting, seeing it all happen again and again, getting up running, running, leaning on a tree and pushing back his head, and breathing slower and slower, until he dozed. And then he would be awakened by a siren or, a racing engine or the echo of gunshots that wouldn't leave his mind, so he started running, running again through the morning mist, and the afternoon fog, and the sharp wind of evening, and the moon coming out and hanging full in the sky, showing all the cracks in the sidewalk and all the paint peeling on doorways, not muting any of the day's secrets.

"Your mama called. You need to call her. She's worried, you know. Everybody's worried."

"I've been running. I just came from where it happened. I've been there every night. The first night everything was closed up. Nobody was standing around, I mean nobody. It didn't even seem like cars were hardly coming by. I went and stood in the doorway I had seen my dad come out of. I stood there thinking, I don't know, thinking if I could see it different maybe I'd wake up, maybe it would turn to last week or fast forward into this week. But now it's a week later, and it's like nothing even happened. D'Prince hanging out with a couple of his boys on the stoop. K.C. in the store smiling at the honeys and snapping at the dogs.

"Tonight I was just standing there, looking at how it was all the same, and then I realized I needed to put a marker up for my Dad. So I reached into my pocket and pulled out one a my pens, a purple one... It's funny because I asked Jimbo to get me a red one, but he said he thought I said purple and black. But the purple, it was just right. I started into making the R. Real big, outlined it in black and was just starting to fill it in when I felt this hand grab my wrist and squeeze so hard I thought my wrist was about to break, and at the same time my mouth was covered, and I'm being pulled down. It was like this phantom just came from outta nowhere and was wrestling me to the ground, and I was tired from running and crying, and Jackie, I didn't have any more fight in me, but I was going to pull some up till I heard this familiar voice in my ear. "Lay low, boy, lay low." And I realize that I'm being held down by some ashy, stringy, bone poking arms.

"I start wrestling and trying to fight, but they got me in this hold and then I see it's Hoodoo. And I smell him, stale urine with a kind of musty, moldy edge, almost like something rotting."

"Who's Hoodoo?"

"My dad's army partner. The one that walks with a limp. I showed him to you once. Anyway, I was cursing and trying to halfway wrestle him offa me, and I start yelling at him "What the fuck, man? What the hell is this?" And he was just holding onto me and we're rolling around the sidewalk, he's holding my arms down, and over and over again, almost singing into my ear,. "Lay low, boy, lay low."

"And then, Jackie, I'm seeing him and my dad the beginning of this year. The two of them, not even seeing me as they walked down the block, just glazed eyes. Hoodoo was trying to look like some curbside kinda style, but my dad, my dad, he was just looking hollow, like he wasn't much more than a puppet shadow. And I realized that now Hoodoo is alive and my dad is...well, I just started tussling. I'm still kicking and finally I pull out an arm and am punching Hoodoo. But he doesn't really fight back. Just tries to hold me back. There I am screaming, Jackie, I'm screaming and crying and hammering on this feeble man, and a crowd gathers around us and is hooting and hollering, and then I feel two arms pulling me off of him.

"It's K.C. 'Easy now, boy, come on, boy, you see he's sick. Easy, boy,' over and over, quiet in my ear. And, Jackie, I've got snot running down my nose, and I can hear the sobs coming from outside of me, and I realize they're my sobs, and, Jackie, I look at Hoodoo and he's just laying there looking up at me. I see he's got an almost clean shirt on, and an old army jacket, and the sweater my grandmother gave him. And, Jackie, he looks at me, and he's got spit and blood coming out of his mouth, and he shakes his head, 'I loved your daddy, boy. You take after him boy, damn near spitting image of him the day I met him. We were both nineteen then. I was just trying to look after you. I didn't mean you no harm. Just trying to stop trouble. I loved your dad, son. Through alla this he never turned his back on me or did me wrong. Not in no real way'

"And then he gets on all fours and crawls over to the

doorway and pulls hisself up. D'Prince reached out to help him but he snatched his arm away. Then Hoodoo straightened out his clothes and wiped the blood from around his nose and just started limping away, muttering about how he loved him, and he woulda been there if he could.

"I realize everyone is staring at me. K.C. is still loosely holding my arms down and I break away from him and start to run again. At first I think I'm running after Hoodoo, but in three and a half seconds I caught up to him and passed him up. I'm crying and running, and I hear this voice at my side, Jackie, clear as I hear you talking to me, or you hear me talking to you. And she says, she tells me I have to stop and sleep. She's right in my ear and I'm trying to act like I don't hear anything. I just keep running, going towards the park. Finally I've got to take a break because my side is hurting and I haven't heard her in awhile, so maybe she, or it, is gone. But no, she's right there, I can almost feel her before she speaks 'You need to sleep, and one a your catnaps over at Victoria's is not going to make it. She's not doing so well since you came by last time. You got a home, find it and find a bed and get in it.' She sounds like somebody's mama hammering out orders. Well, I catch my breath and get ready to start off again, and there that voice is, 'I know you hear me, boy, what you think I'm a fool?' I don't know if she's not a fool or not, I sure as hell know I must be some kinda crazy."

Jackie smiled, "You got to tell this revelation to Dawa."

For the first time since that night Sketch smiled. "She already knows the part about me being crazy. But on the real, Jackie, I just keep hearing this voice telling me I have to stop and sleep. Said I couldn't run forever."

"So I say to myself, out loud, but to myself. "I can sure as hell try." And damned if that voice don't start laughing so hard it starts wheezing. And I decide to take off to Oakland. Maybe she won't follow me there. Well, I reach the BART train and get on a middle car, and start through it with her at my elbow. "Sit down, boy. Rest your eyes." But after we reach the last San Francisco station, she's gone. I can feel it, but just to be sure I keep walking through a couple more cars, and I'm seeing women put their purse straps back on their shoulders and hold them closer. And I'm seeing men sit up a little taller and pretend to look hard straight in front of them, but I can see my reflection in the corner of their eyes. And, Jackie, I got off the train at McArthur, and I didn't know where to go, but I know I need to stop. I need to stop. So I came here, Jackie. Just for a minute, girl. Just for a minute."

"Come on and go upstairs. If you're kinda quick about it, you can take a shower. I'll bring you a towel and some of my brother's clothes. Make sure you bring the towel in my room. Don't leave it in the bathroom."

Sketch just stood still. Jackie took his hand and pulled hard. This time he followed her inside.

Later that night, Jackie went up to her room. There was Sketch lying on his back, his eyes wide open and staring at the ceiling. He had on her brother's baggy jeans and an oversized t-shirt. She could see scratches on his face and a slight swelling under one eye.

"Whatcha doing awake, Jamalman?" she said softly, coming close to the bed.

"You ever seen anybody die, Jackie?"

"Once. We were all there when my great-grandmother passed. Mama, Duane, two uncles, all three of my aunts, my grandpa. It was kinda nice actually. We even had family up from Arkansas, and my cousins from New York. She was like the grand matriarch. My aunt Melanie has a beautiful voice and she was singing different old timey blues songs. In fact, her and Uncle Tim got in an argument. He said she should only be singing songs that praised the Lord at a moment like this, and Grandmama, she told him to shush. Said she wanted her niece to sing whatever pleased her. In fact, told her to sing some raunchy Bessie Smith. I tell you my Dad cracked up. And Tim he shut his mouth and frowned, but Melanie she just went back to her humming. Folks were sitting around quietly telling stories, and Grandmama just like let go, you know. Just let go. That's how I want to go, old as the hills, and surrounded by love. I tell you, that's the way."

"Not like my dad."

"From what I heard, he was surround by love, Jamalman."

"Jackie, he just stood there. He coulda ducked, he coulda ran, he coulda just stepped one way or the other. But he just stood there frozen like he'd been waiting for it. Like it was the place where he needed to be. He lived through a war, and he couldn't dodge some fire that wasn't even aiming at him?"

Sketch started to cry again. Slow, hard sobs. Jackie sat on the edge of the bed and tried to rub his back. He pulled away. She stretched out next to him and wrapped her arms around him. She began to hum in his ear so softly he could barely here the tune. "It'll be alright Jamalman, It'll be alright."

"Nothing is going to be alright."

"You're going to be alright, Jamalman. You're going to be alright."

She hummed and chanted and rocked Jamal until finally he could no longer fight it, and he sank into a dark, dreamless sleep. The next morning, before it was completely light, Jamal got up and slipped out of Jackie's house. No one heard him go. And only the garbage men lifting heavy cans onto their shoulders saw him as he began to stretch his legs and run down Ruby Street back towards San Francisco.

15. Jet Black

I knew from the start that Jamal Sketch Everman wasn't going to the funeral. I knew because of the way he talked to Victoria about anything but his father's actual dying. Oh, he had plenty to say about the moments before the shooting, but he never breathed a sigh about seeing his dad fall, or seeing him actually pass on, at the hospital. He stopped in at Victoria's about every day up to the funeral. The day before the funeral he actually looked like he'd slept in the park. His eyes were red and his voice was real soft. He came a different time every day. He'd knock soft, soft but persistent. Then he would start to call out her name. Victoria would pretend she wasn't going to answer the door, but after awhile she'd get up and let him in.

She would make tea and fix a plate of cookies, and he would ask again about that night. And even when he was asking Victoria about that night, again and again, even when he was trying to help her fill in the colors, the shape of the car, the hue of the shooter's skin, it seemed to me that he didn't seem to want to look too hard at how his father died, or why the man was at that store in the first place. Seemed like Sketch heard, but didn't hear what Victoria decided to say to him.

Ever since those young men had taunted her on the street, Victoria had taken a turning. She was afraid to go out. She stayed in most of the time and hardly ate a bite. So I guess she kind of liked having someone besides me to talk to. Still, she seemed to be more and more tired every day. She kept going on about how she couldn't get her shields back up. I knew she had decided to let go, to move on. Of course I didn't know then that she wasn't going on any more walks. So I can't say I really appreciated Sketch coming by and bothering us, until afterwards.

And you know, she let him in every single time. And every time he came she told him a story about growing up in the city. And at the end of the conversation, every time, Sketch would ask her to explain again what the light looked like coming out of his father. Did it have colors? Did it pour like liquid, or was it more like rays of color shooting out a diamond? Victoria got impatient sometimes, "Boy, you felt the light in your own hands. You poured it back into his body. I saw you. What did it feel like to you? You saw it, you had to. How else could you have pushed some back in?" Sometimes when he would ask her again, she just got up without a word and went back into her bedroom. She would take off her shoes and lie on top of her covers with all her clothes on and not move again until the next morning.

One time, after Victoria left the room, Sketch dozed off for about two hours. Finally I had to ask him to move, "Don't you think you should be going?" I said as calm as I could. Frankly, the boy was getting on my nerves. He shoots straight up and then pretends like he's calling out to Victoria, "I guess I should be going," but I know he's answering me. That's when I started following him, watching him return over and over to that storefront. I knew he couldn't get any of it right in his head till he stopped and slept some. Even then it couldn't get all the way right because sometimes things just don't go right, they go crooked, and round the backside, and inside out. You just don't always get what you think is sposed to happen. Well, I can tell you. That Jamal didn't want to hear a word I had to say. He couldn't keep hisself from hearing, but he sure could keep hisself from listening. And he did, just kept his ears full of wind rushing by.

So Jamal stayed away for a couple of weeks. When he finally did come to visit again, Victoria wasn't receiving. See, Victoria didn't have her makeup on, and she wasn't going to open the door. But that boy he just was so persistent, knocking and calling out, "Miss Cheevers! Miss Cheevers, I've got a present for you! I found some light for you! Miss Cheevers!"

Well, first off Victoria tried to go in the back of the apartment, but of course she could still hear him. Then she tried to put her hands over her ears, but she could still hear him and could feel the door shaking. That boy was not going away on his own. He would have to be sent away. I went out and told him to "Get on," in as loud a voice as I could muster. Hard-headed child just stood there like he hadn't heard a thing. Oh, I saw the hairs give a rise on the back of his neck, and saw a little bit of sweat raise on his upper lip, but he just shook those little dreadlocks and kept on, "Miss Cheevers, just let me give this present to you. It's full of light. I know you'll like it." Finally Victoria gave in, and, even though she wasn't made-up, answered the door.

"Jamal Everman, you are insufferably rude," she said on opening the door.

"Yes, ma'am. Good afternoon. You look very nice today, Miss Cheevers."

"I am not even properly dressed, young man."

"But you look—you look glowing today, Miss Cheevers. You are not that much lighter than my mama. Kind of a sandy tan to her cinnamon. You're more yellow and she's kind of red."

"Young man, I do not believe I asked you to analyze me or my skin colors. They are not what matters. All that matters is the light. Why are you bothering me anyway? When a person does not answer the door, it indicates that the person does not welcome callers."

"May I come in?"

I say right up in his ear, "If she'd a wanted you in, she'd a invited you in."

Of course, he's got his head up in a tree, doesn't pay nary a mind to me or wait for Victoria's invite. No. He just walks on in. Now, I swear, I have never so much wished I had some arms to push that young man out, or a strong leg to give him a kick in the behind. But I couldn't, so he moved right on past me.

"I brought you a present. I saw it in one of the windows of a thrift store." Victoria walked over to the sofa, and Sketch sat down next to her.

"Would you like a cup of tea, young man?"

Now I noticed that Sketch didn't really like tea. I mean the way he always loaded it up with sugar was sure to kill the flavor. "No, thank you, Miss Cheevers, I didn't come to trouble you."

"Well, if you did not come to trouble me, why were you banging on the door so?"

With that, Victoria got up, walked into the kitchen, and began to boil some water. Sketch followed her. He pulled a small package out of the breast pocket of his loose plaid shirt. It was folded in white tissue paper. "I've been thinking about what you keep telling me about the light, Miss Cheevers; then I realized that white doesn't pull the light. It pushes it away. It's like it's afraid of it, and it puts a wall up against it. Black pulls the light. It sucks it in, and then it lets it out in all the colors you can imagine."

With that, he unwrapped a pretty black brooch that was cut in an oval with sloping sides. It shined bright as could be, and you could see all kinds of purples and reds and yellows leaping off of it, as it caught the corners of the sun coming in through the kitchen window.

"See, Miss Cheevers. This is jet. There's nothing more black than jet. But look at it. It's warm and all full of the light."

"A diamond gives you more colors."

"And what's a diamond born outta, Miss Cheevers? Coal. And where's it live? Down in the center of the earth. I'm telling you, Miss Cheevers, look at all of this light!" He held up the brooch again. At that moment the kettle started to whistling, and Victoria rushed on over. I could see her hands were trembling. Sketch saw her hands flutter and reached past Victoria and turned off the stove. Then he caught her hands, "Miss Cheevers, I just wanted to give you this."

He took her hand and put the brooch inside. I couldn't believe it. She let him just touch her like that and didn't say a word. Then she walked back into the living room and sat down on the sofa. "I'm not used to getting presents, young man. Not used to it at all." It was then I realized that Victoria's eyes were all full of tears. "Why are you giving me this, child?"

"Everyone talks about my father, talking about how they always knew he was going to come to this, about how even when he was young he wasn't this or he wasn't that, but you, you didn't even know him, but still you saw him full of light. You saw him as something more than just some kind of crackhead. You saw him as I knew he was, inside. And this jet, Miss Cheevers, this jet, it's like my dad. Shiny and full of light."

"I think you should go now, son," Victoria said. "I thank you for your present."

"Put it on, Miss Cheevers," Sketch quietly said. "Put it on and watch it shine on you." Victoria's hands were still trembling, and she dropped the brooch on the floor.

"Can I help you? I help my grandmother put her pins on lots of times. Her fingers get cramped from arthritis sometimes, and I help her."

Victoria didn't say a word. Sketch bent over, picked up the brooch, and opened it. Then he pinned it right under the collar of Victoria's blouse, so that it rested at the middle of her collarbones. "Now that black, sitting in the middle of all that white you're wearing, Miss Cheevers, I believe it'll bring you even more light," Sketch smiled.

"I do believe it really is time for you to go, son." Victoria said again very quietly, her hands fluttering up to her neck, covering up the black pin.

"Me, too," I said.

"Hush now," Victoria said to me, but Sketch acted like she was talking to him,

"Wasn't going to say anything, Miss Cheevers. But you look nice. Really. I'll come check on you soon." And then he walked himself right out that door. Victoria, she took herself into the bedroom, and laid herself across the covers and just put her hands over her throat and held that brooch all day long.

I stayed with her until she fell asleep, and then I went out to the beach. Of course, I knew I'd find Sketch there. I went right on over to him. He was just a working with his pens and little paint cans. Making him a whole picture wall. By the time I got there he was covered with sweat. By the time I caught up with him, the sun had dropped below the horizon and shadows hung across the wall that Sketch was covering. This was for his father, this was for himself. Sketch worked quickly, but carefully. From time to time, he wiped the tears away that were streaming down his face, used his sleeve to dry his running nose.

Usually Sketch was very particular about how he dressed. He liked everything to be coordinated, from oversized shirt, hanging down in a complimentary shade, to wide-legged pants. A knit cap usually covering the dreadlocks he was just beginning to grow. Dawa always teased him about his neatness, declaring that he couldn't be a real artist if he was afraid to get paint on himself. Sketch would laugh at her most of the time. "Paints are supposed to go on the walls, Auntie, not my clothes."

"Paints are supposed to go on a canvas or paper or something, Sketch, not other people's walls," she'd answer.

I saw an outline real faint in the corner of what I knew was going to turn out to be Victoria. It was right over the horse that young lady had drawn just a couple of weeks before. And then near his own name there was an outline that was sure to be turned into his father. Soon as he had finished the outline, he stopped, and then sunk into the sand, crying.

Thing is, Lucille and Sketch they wanted to see Ranger all one kind of way, and most other folks wanted to see him all the way another, like Mitch. Mitch didn't have a good word to say. And neither side was all the way fair. But there were lots of ways to see him, I know because I saw him turn into different people like a chameleon. And a whole lot of those folks was people you would not want to be caught with in a dark alley. I'm here to tell you it wasn't all that simple. I mean everyone has to live their own life and make their own choices. One thing I know, from the time I came to know that man, it was like he couldn't believe in anything. Oh yeah, he had his dashiki and his Afro and his Africa medallion, like everybody else. He even put some time in at the Black Man's Free Clinic. You should have seen Victoria when they put the sign up for that place. She thought it was so improper, Negroes calling themselves Black. She stood aside for African, but she turned her nose up at *black*, I tell you. She said black was darkness, and darkness was away from the light, and away from the light was wrong. That was that. But even inside the clinic there was some people with wrong thinking, trying to pass off the game as a new kind of politics.

"Everybody is corrupt," Ranger'd say. "It's just a matter of what it takes to show it. Even them damn monks burning themselves up on the streets. All of them got something rotten inside." But folks tried to show him different. Even me, not that he cared a whit about me, or even knew I was there for that matter, but I think he suspected something. I'd try to get him to turn around sometimes, to catch sight of the something good that always be happening right next to the something ugly. Every once in a while he'd hear when I called his name, and start to turn around, but then, like he'd been cautioned by one of the old ones not to answer, he'd just get all stiff, and keeps his eyes on whatever he was looking into. So he missed the signs that might have helped him get on over. He was always looking the wrong way because he just didn't know when to turn around, and when to stay the course. It wasn't like Lucille said at all, blaming everybody but Ranger. And it wasn't like Sketch saw either. I have a lot of respect, but I just don't think no one was seeing him all the way.

It was getting on to dusk when Sketch packed up his tools and started to walk towards the park. I decided to walk with him, but also decided to keep my peace since he wasn't paying me any mind anyway. Then that boy, from this slow, heavy-footed walk, starts to running. Now Sketch don't hardly have a smile in him except when he's running. Even when he's painting he's all frowned up. Not like Ranger, one thing I can say about him, if you were in any kind of a slump, he had some kind of word to make you smile. Didn't have too many for himself, but he sure had plenty to share. Well, here's Sketch just running through the trees and getting all out of breath and making me work to keep up with him. Finally, after about what had to be ten, twelve city blocks, he slows down and decides to sit on an empty bench off to the side of this meadow.

There was Sketch, wet and clammy, his shirt wrinkled, shadows under his eyes, spread across a bench. His head hung backwards, and he seemed to be laid out in an open prayer underneath the smooth blue sky. And there was Mitch driving slow, looking for his stepson. Mitch saw Sketch as he turned the curve of the road. He sat in the car for some minutes just watching. Sketch didn't seem to notice the man. After he had completely caught his breath, Sketch got back up, and began to run again.

Mitch got out of the car and caught up with him. This time Sketch saw Mitch, but he didn't stop running. Mitch and he ran next to each other for a couple of blocks. Mitch began to get winded and called out, "Jamal, hold up for a minute. Just a minute, son."

Sketch stopped. "You're not my father."

Mitch shook his head, "Boy, I've been calling you son

since before I even knew who your mother was. Don't pull an attitude with me."

"What you want?"

"Everyone is worried about you. Your mother is all tied up in knots, your grandmother is sitting up by the window all night every night. Dawa is walking the streets cursing everyone she sees. Ruben tells me she's even got that old white lady looking for you."

Sketch had to laugh at that. "Dawa got Miss Cheevers after me? Now that's something. That lady isn't going to tell Dawa anything. I've just been running, Mitch. Haven't bothered nobody. You know I've been bunking with this friend and that one. I know Mama knows. I've got the messages. And I know she got mine. Tommy G. told me he called her. I know Jackie called her. I just didn't have anything to say. Just been running, and drawing, and thinking."

"You want to run, why don't you get on a team?"

"I don't want to race. I just want to run. I start when I want. I stop when I want. I run for me."

"I'm just saying you could do something with it."

"Mitch, what do you want?" Sketch said, with an edge of exasperation.

"I want you to come on home and talk to your mother. I want you to get it together and help your grandmother out. You missed the funeral..."

"Didn't miss nothing."

"And then too, the police are looking for you too. They said that you were there when your father got shot, and they are trying to find who did it. They want to question you about what you saw, who you saw."

"I saw my father get hit. And then I ran to the hospital and I saw him just after he died, too. Saw M'dear holding him and then saw him fall all limp. And I saw M'dear just singing. I didn't go in. Didn't want to talk to old Elise. Didn't want to talk to anyone."

"First time you saw somebody die, son?"

"I've seen dead people before."

"I used to hunt with my uncle when I was a boy. We brought down deer and rabbits and ducks. I was pretty good with a shotgun. Then I went off to war and saw plenty of body bags, but it was a while until I saw somebody die. It was my bunk buddy, Fremont. You know he had buttoned his damn shirt wrong, and when he died, I noticed that the buttons were off. You know I sat there and unbuttoned his shirt, and rebuttoned it up right. Damn war going on around me and I'm worrying about this man looking neat in a body bag."

"That doesn't sound like you."

"You don't know me, Jamal. Besides, it is me."

"I guess it is. It's the shipshape, everything-in-order part, that's you."

"All of it's me. It was like I wasn't sure he was really dead. I thought maybe, maybe... Half his damn head was blown off. But I didn't really see it. I didn't let myself see it. All I saw was the middle of his shirt bulging out and the buttons all off."

"You got a point to this?"

"It's not something you want to go through alone, Jamal. Not if you don't have to."

"Yeah, man. Well, now you saw me, so you can tell Mama and M'dear I'm fine. I'll be home soon enough. I'm getting on now."

Sketch started running again.

Mitch called out, "You can't run forever, son."

Sketch stopped and turned around. "Mitch, I'm not bothering anybody. I'm not breaking your laws or anybody else's. I'm just thinking things through." He turned back and began to walk away in long easy strides. Mitch caught up with him,

"Your mother wants me take you to DC. Seems your father had these bus tickets. Now I want to be on a bus for four days with you about as much as you want to be on one with me. But I tell you what, son. We don't even have to sit together. You can run up and down that bus aisle long as the driver lets you. But your mother and Dawa are going to fuss at me until we go."

"I'll think about it."

"I got time off for the trip week after next."

"I said 'I'll think about it.' "

"I'll leave your ticket at your grandmother's house. Bring a change or two of clothes. And take a bath, boy. You smell like sweat and dirt."

"And you smell like stale cigars."

Mitch put his hand on Sketch's shoulders. "You look like you could use a meal. Come on in for a landing, son."

Sketch was still breathing hard, "You don't know how much it hurts."

"Jamal, you have no idea what I know and don't know." Mitch shook his head. "I've lost some friends. I've lost some family. And I've been there. Your mother needs you. Your grandmother needs you. Jamal, come on home."

Sketch looked at Mitch, held his eyes. Mitch was calm and didn't move a muscle. He didn't reach out to the boy, and he didn't pull away his eyes. He wasn't trying to get into Sketch's head either, the way some folks do when they are looking inside. He just was looking, just seeing the boy all full of knots and confusion. And funny, for Mitch that is, he wasn't judging either, just looking.

I just couldn't resist. I leaned over and whispered into Sketch's ear, "You father wants you to do this, boy."

"I know my father wants me to do it," he answered real sharp. Mitch was kind of taken aback because he hadn't said anything. Well, you know, Mitch'll have to live at least three, four more lifetimes before he can hear a body like me. But Mitch, I got to give it to him, he doesn't miss a lick, "Come on in, boy. Come on in." Then Mitch he put his arm around the boy, and turned him around, and the two of them walked back to the car.

Mitch opened the door and kinda gently pushed Sketch into the front seat. Sketch collapsed in the seat. I had to squeeze on in quick before Mitch slammed the door shut and rushed around to the driver's side like he was afraid Sketch might change his mind and jump out if he didn't get the car started straight away. Mitch fastened his seat belt, and I could see he wanted to tell Sketch to fasten his, too. He even started to reach over to fasten it for him, but then he thought better and let it go. We three rode back to Lucille's house. When Mitch pulled up, Sketch turned to him,

"You don't have to come up. I'll go on in. What day we leaving?"

"Your mother wants to see you."

"I'll check in. I'll call her soon as I get inside. What day we going?"

"A week from Friday."

"What time?"

"I'll pick you up at 8 in the morning."

"I'll be ready."

Sketch got out the car and started to walk towards the stairs. Mitch got out too. Sketch turned around. "Mitch, it's okay. Thank you. I'll call Mama. I need to stay in the city right now. But I'll be ready a week from Friday. Thanks, man—really.'

Mitch shook his head but didn't say another word. Then he just got back in the car and drove away. Me, I went on back to Victoria. She was still lying there, clutching that brooch, her face all streaked with the salt from dried tears. She didn't even acknowledge me when I came in, didn't say a word. She just continued to lie there, fully dressed, holding that pin and staring out the window into the night that was slowly coming down.

16. Buses and Cars

When Friday morning came, Jamal boarded the bus with Mitch. His mother hugged him so tightly that he was sure she left welts on his arms. Lucille had loaded them down with fried chicken, a pound cake, a bag of fruit, and a thermos full of ice tea. Dawa had laughed at her, "Mama, Jim Crow is over. They can eat at the restaurants on the way."

"I know that, Cheryl Lynn. When's the last time you saw some good food near a bus station that wasn't brought from home?"

Jamal leaned over and kissed his grandmother. "Thank you, M'dear. I might even share some of it with Mitch."

Mitch did not crack a smile as he said, "Then you might even get home in one piece."

Everyone was relieved that Jamal was going on the trip. He even offered the edge of a smile for the occasion, mugging at his aunt as the bus pulled out of the station. The ride across the country was uneventful. The good food ran out the end of the first day, and dry burgers with greasy fries, beers for Mitch, and colas for Jamal were food for the next three days. For the first couple of days, Mitch tried to engage Jamal in conversation. He talked about the first trip he had ever taken away from home, a trip south to meet his father's family, who still owned land in the swamps of Louisiana. "Right on the bayou, son. Not good for much but fishing and taking tourists on boat rides. But beautiful. Can't farm it, but I tell you it's a wonderland. Your father woulda loved that land. You could just smell life in the air when the wind blows, life and death."

Jamal mostly grunted responses and doodled in his sketch book. When Mitch was asleep, Jamal drew a pencil drawing of the man's head, broad jaw, flat forehead, thick even lips, deep creases at the edges of his eyes and, even as he slept, deep creases across his eyebrows, like his face was set in a permanent scowl. When Mitch was awake, all he ever saw Jamal drawing was tags of Ranger's name. Each had a different style, sometimes curves and swirls and sometimes block letters. Sometimes the letters filled a quarter of the page, but most times they were cramped up and small. By the time they reached D.C., Sketch had filled the notebook.

They arrived in the late afternoon with plenty of daylight hours left. As soon as they got off the bus, Jamal started asking about the monument. "Let's go there directly. It can't be that far."

"Center of D.C.'s not all that big, son, nothing is that far. But right now we're going to get a shower and some fresh clothes," Mitch responded.

Mitch checked them into a small hotel near the station. Jamal was in and out of the shower in five minutes. He dressed in some oversized khakis and one of his father's old white shirts. Mitch, on the other hand, took a long time to bathe. He enjoyed the feeling of the water rolling down his back and took the time to rinse off four days of sour conversations with Jamal. Jamal paced the room and cursed under his breath as Mitch got ready in his usual fastidious manner. He even polished his shoes.

"Man, we going to a memorial, not a party," Jamal had fumed.

"I got a whole lot of friends whose names are up there, son. I think I'll give them some respect, and I think you will too."

Jamal gulped in some air, "Sorry, man, really, sorry. I just want to get there."

"You aren't the only one lost people. Everyone you see on these streets lost somebody. And a whole lot of us lost them in war. And as for being in a hurry, I believe I've been waiting to see this wall a lot more years than you." Mitch looked at himself in the wide mirror that rested on top of the hotel-room dresser. “But I think I am ready. Let’s go.”

“’Bout time,” Sketch whispered under his breath.

Mitch didn’t say another word to Jamal. The two of them got into a cab and rode to the monument. Mitch’s hands were sweating, and he was surprised as he opened the sheet of folded paper that he had taken from his pocket as they got out of the taxi. It was moist around the edges as he unfolded it. He had eight of his own names to look up, and three more he was looking up for Ranger.

Mitch stopped on the edge of the walk, not yet ready to walk down to the monument. He looked into Jamal’s eyes, “The last time I saw your father we talked about this place. ‘Man,’ he said, ‘Man, soon as I get my act all the way together, Sketch and I are going to that wall and we going to make sure they remembered Maddog and Simba right.’ Yeah, the last time I saw your father...”

Mitch started to walk down the walk with Jamal at his side. They approached the monument from its backside. Its top edge could barely be seen, shining, a smoky black against the crisp green of the lawns that surrounded it. As they walked to the north side, Mitch stopped at the podium which was an almanac of names. He had the list that Jeannine had insisted he bring. Not the names that showed their souls, the way they fought, the way they dreamed, not Record Man, Hawkeye, and Red, but the names that held their families and cut out a corner of their ancestors’ history, Jerome Griffin, George Williams, Yancey Dupree. The only one he ever called by his given name was Jefferson, Jefferson Davis, named in cynical revenge by his father, who was going to have white teachers stare into his son’s midnight face, every day, and call out his name like he was a Confederate hero. When teachers tried to call his name out as Jeff, he wouldn’t answer. “My name is Jefferson Davis,” he would say. “I’m the one who won the war.” And then the class would laugh.

Mitch mumbled something to himself, and then turned

to the book and began to seek out the names. James Bell was first. 1970. He was the first close friend of Mitch's to die. So Mitch was the one who stayed up that long restless night writing to James's mother, telling her what she already knew, that her son had courage, that her son was a noble man, that her son was a good friend to have, that her son was loved, and that her son was dead. Mitch's hand trembled as he found the name and the panel date when he died, 1970. "December," Mitch spat out. "One sorry-ass Christmas, one mean New Year." Mitch didn't notice Sketch move away. As Sketch moved to the far end of the wall, Mitch leafed through the pages. Jefferson Davis, Jesus Garcia, Anthony Green, Joseph Kim.

Sketch stood at the last panel and saw his father's eyes staring back at him from the expanse of smooth marble, missing the names of those who were killed in battle but did not die until years later. Names like his father, Elliott Everman Junior. Sketch had practiced for the week before. He knew, as soon as he thought of it, that he could do it. He would pull the small stencil from the right pocket with one hand, and the silver paint from the other with the left, shield his back from the monument, and use his forefinger to hold back the side of the jacket with the other. He'd gotten it down to five seconds with no smears.

Sketch looked around. At the far end of the monument, under 1959, a small white woman was putting down a vase with what looked to be some flowers in it. Both hands were full of the flowers. She knelt and put one in front of the Wall. Her hair was silver-gray, and she had on a pale blue suit and darker blue hat. She was dressed as if for church, Sketch thought. A man stood further down rubbing a chalk across a piece of paper to get an imprint of a name. Ranger's name wouldn't be engraved, but it would be there. Sketch took a breath; this was the moment. There were no security guards to be seen, the park was quiet, Mitch was engrossed, and everyone was circling inside their own tiny universe, as

Sketch pulled the small can out and pressed the neat stencil against the wall. "1989—Ranger E," it read. Sketch had carved the letters with an exacto knife creating his own letter design. It was not the regimented clean type of the other names, but a tag which circled clearly through its three and one-half inches. The R resembled a leaf to a tree, the A was engulfed by the N which scooped up the G which looked like the barrel of a gun. The E and R lay on top of each other, looking almost like an eyebrow arching over a half-shut eye. The final E was larger, giving the feeling of an exclamation mark. Sketch held his breath, and did not realize that tears were streaming down his face. He sprayed the name on the wall, and then smoothly circled away.

Jamal moved to the edge of the monument and put the spray can in the garbage. Then he pocketed the stencil, and walked towards Mitch, who was just leaving the podium. Mitch had found the location of the last name on his list and was walking toward Sketch. "Come on, boy," he said, throwing his arm around Sketch's shoulder. "Let's find some names."

He pulled Sketch around the lawn, "Start at the beginning and go through the year," Mitch said. Sketch wiped his face and allowed himself to be led. "Not so many in '59," Mitch said as they looked at the names. "It was still unofficial then." The old woman Jamal had noticed before quietly replied, "Too many," as if the comment had been directed at her. Mitch looked at the woman's face, resigned, yet deeply sad, and touched her shoulder, "Yes, ma'am, too many." The woman drew aside sharply, and only afterwards looked into Mitch's eyes which were swollen with the memories of his own loss. She was about to speak, but the words clawed across her teeth. Then they came out in little slivers of glass from her thin dry lips, "My husband and my son, and one of my brothers, and his best friend. It was their *career* choice, a *family* tradition. My father was a captain, thirty-seven years of service, before he retired. The Marsh family is a fighting family. That's what we always said. And here's our reward." She moved down the monument and stopped at 1963. She knew exactly where the name was carved that she wanted to read once more. She ran her fingers across it, and then kneeled as she had done many times before, and placed a flower at the foot of the wall.

Mitch and Sketch moved down the wall, calling out the names of people they had never known. "Look, here's a woman," Jamal called out, "Didn't know they had women fighting there." Mitch frowned as he looked at the name, "Dying, not fighting. Probably was a nurse. You can be pretty sure she saved a whole lot of lives before they got her." Jamal kept walking and reading names, wiping away the last remnants of the tears that were in his eyes, "Lookie here. Hey, I didn't know Chinese fought in the war. I wondered how it felt killing folks that look like you, but live thousands of miles away."

"I'm not sure that killing folks anywhere is all that much different," said Mitch. "But that's a Korean name, Jamal." Every time Mitch reached a name, he stopped and said a silent prayer. When they reached the last panel, Mitch saw Sketch's work. The old woman had reached the panel a few minutes earlier and stood there enraged. "WHY?" she asked, "Why would someone deface a national monument? Why?" As Mitch pulled the boy from the wall he turned to the woman, "Maybe that was their way of remembering someone. The wrong way, but their way."

Mitch quickly led Sketch to the curb, where he flagged down a cab, and pushed him into the car. As Sketch hit the back seat, Mitch's hand flew out and hit Sketch in the jaw.

"What in the hell is wrong with you? Do you know how much time you could do for that? This isn't the side of some store in a broke-down neighborhood. Boy, this is the goddamn Vietnam Memorial! What were you thinking?"

The cab driver turned around. "Man, you got a destination, or do you just want us to ride around while you talk to your boy?"

"Yeah, take us to the bus station."

"You went to see the monument, huh?" the cabbie continued with a thick accented voice, "When it first went up, I wasn't too impressed, but I've seen it a bunch of times now. I got to say that girl had some kinda idea who built it. Makes you remember what it's all about. A lot of people died in that war. In every war." The man was toasted almond and his skin glowed in red. He came from elsewhere.

"You from Africa?" Sketch asked, ignoring Mitch.

"No, boy. I'm Haitian. My great-great-grandfather fought with Dessalines. I come from fighting people."

"But now you drive a cab."

"It's just a pass-through, boy. Just a pass-through."

They rode the rest of the way in silence. As they got out the cab, Mitch pulled Sketch away from the steps. "Let's walk." After two blocks Mitch said, "It's going to be on the news, you know. I need to turn your black ass in. Where do you get off?"

"Man, you're not going to turn me in. I know what I was doing. His name deserved to be up there. His name and a whole lot more. Dawa said..."

"You know I don't give a damn what Dawa said."

"Mitch, everybody says I never really knew my dad. Everybody says the man he was died somewhere in Vietnam, that the one who came back wasn't the same person. Where's his monument, Mitch? Where's my father's monument?"

Mitch saw a barber shop and collared Sketch and pulled him inside. The barber, shears in hand, yelled out, "I don't allow no mess up in here."

Mitch ignored him and pulled Sketch to the mirror. As the barber moved away from his customer, about to throw Mitch and Sketch out of the shop, he heard Mitch saying, "Where's your father's fuckin Vietnam monument? There!" He pointed at Sketch. "Stand up straight with your poop-butt self, going to show everybody you somebody, putting your name on this bus, and that grocery store, and the other garage, like everybody need to see what you decide they're supposed to see. You the damn monument. Got his long jaw, stand close to as tall as him, walk with his gait. About the only piece of your mama that I see is your eyes. You're the one that keeps it going, not some damn piece of marble."

For the second time that day Sketch's eyes filled with tears. This time, though, he was aware of a shop full of strangers watching his stepfather and him. "Alright, man," he softly said, hoping to quiet Mitch down. "Alright, man."

Mitch let go of Sketch's collar and straightened out his own jacket. "Sorry to disrupt," he said, ushering Sketch to the door. "I beg your pardon. You folks have a good day." The barber shook his head and returned to his customer, "You want me to cut a line in?"

Mitch checked them back out of the hotel, and they got back on the bus that evening to go home. Mitch picked up a newspaper when the bus crossed through Chicago. In small print hidden away was a note that the Vietnam monument had been defaced, but was already sanded down and returned to its former glory. It noted that Ranger was a common nickname, and it was unlikely that the vandal would be found. The security guard assigned to that side of the monument had been fired. Mitch was going to show the article to Jamal, but decided not to. He reasoned that "the fool boy might get off the bus and hitchhike back to do it again."

When they arrived back in the city and got off the bus, Jamal grabbed his bag and yelled to Mitch that he would catch the streetcar to his grandmother's house. Mitch caught him by the shoulder, and pulled him towards the car Jeannine had waiting. "No, boy, I think you'll be staying with your mom and me for awhile. I kept your behind out of jail, and you owe me. So you just come on home. Matter of fact, I got some work for you, you love painting so. We're going to repaint the house, room by room. I do the buying of the supplies, and you do the painting. You can start with your brother and sister's room."

Just then Jeannine walked up and gave Mitch a long hug. Evie and Michael had jumped out of the back seat of the car. Evie's arm was in a cast and sling. Michael was sporting a black eye. Mitch leaned over and lightly cuffed his son on the ear. The words started spilling out of the thirteen-year-old boy, who puffed up and raised his voice, ready to fight again, "Who you been boxing, boy?"

"Stupid punks thought they was going to take my shoes. I had them in the locker at the pool and when I came to get dressed, this boy had pulled my shoes out, and was fixin to put them on. So I fired him up."

"Looks like he won."

Michael held up his foot with the almost new running shoe that he had helped to pay for, "I got my shoes, and you haven't seen him."

Then he turned to Jamal. "I did just like you said. I just held on and didn't let go. I was with Jeremy. He grabbed my shoes and I just kept swinging. The guy wasn't that tough. Only got one good hit."

"Yeah, man, I see that," Jamal let out a corner of a smile, "I think you and me might need to work a little more on the blocking, though."

Mitch turned to Jeannine, "And what about Evie?"

"I fell off my bike. I was riding with no hands and then..."

Mitch picked up Evie and motioned to Jamal to get the luggage. "Woman, I leave you for one week and things fall apart."

"Your car ain't wrecked, your house ain't burnt down, and I decided not to leave you for that fine millionaire lives up on the hill. I think you best be happy. But I'm glad you're back. How'd the trip go?"

Everyone piled into the car. Jamal mumbled that it was

alright and tried to change the subject. But his mother wouldn't let up, "You two are back a couple of days early. Why?"

"Your son didn't take to DC. too well." Mitch said teeth set hard. "Ain't that right, boy."

"Liked it fine, man. I liked it fine."

When they got out of the car, both Jamal and Mitch moved to the trunk. Michael offered to carry Jamal's bag. "Go on in," Jamal said, "I need to talk to your father."

Jeannine pulled Evie and Michael down the walkway towards the front door.

"Mitch, I just...," Jamal paused, at a loss for words. "You alright, man. I mean, thank you. For taking me and for ..." Jamal stood there his mouth open, and no words falling out, "You alright, man."

"Yeah, well, you got a hell of a lot of growing to do, boy," Mitch said, and threw his arm around Jamal. "A hell of a lot of growing to do." Then he handed Jamal both suitcases and walked up the stairs. "And you can start about now."

Jamal shook his head, smiling, "Now ain't this a..."

Mitch turned back gruffly, "You got something to say?"

"No, man, just glad you don't weigh a few more pounds or this case would really be heavy."

Mitch looked up at the house. "What you think, boy, after we get the inside of the house done, maybe you can start on the garage."

"Now that's an idea, Mitch. I got a piece I've been wanting to put on the garage. See it starts with a tree..."

"Son, you out of your mind if you think I'm going to let you mess up my garage," Mitch said. "We're talking a white door and some brown trim."

"Naw, Mitch, listen. I could really do something slamming on the wall..." Jamal smiled broadly as the two men walked inside.

17. On the Beach

It's strange now, not being with Victoria. She died just a few weeks after Sketch got back from his trip. He came to see her one more time. He stood at the door and banged and called, but she couldn't get up. Her niece came down after a while and told him to go away. She scoffed at him when he told her that Victoria was his friend. "My aunt doesn't have any friends, just family," that silly woman said. But Sketch, he stood his ground, said he'd given her a brooch for her last birthday. Well, I knew it wasn't for her birthday, but Sheila didn't, and Sheila had seen the stone on her aunt's dress. That Victoria, every time she changed clothes, and then later when she got really weak and Sheila had to help her, every time she insisted that she be wearing the brooch. Well, Sheila had seen the brooch, and humored her, unpinning and repinning it every day, but she still wouldn't let the boy inside. Later when Sheila finally had the ambulance folks come and carry Victoria over to the hospital, she still wouldn't tell Sketch where the woman was.

It was a Thursday evening, and Sheila was busy cleaning out Victoria's place. The woman wasn't even dead yet, and here her niece was already sweeping and opening windows and carrying out Victoria's little trinkets. Sketch walked up and asked about Victoria, and Sheila answered, "She's gone." Well, she *was* gone, because she wasn't there, but she sure wasn't dead yet. So I told Sketch the truth. Just came right up to him. "Don't jump out your skin, " I said, "She's getting ready to cross over, but she isn't gone yet. She's at county hospital on the sixth floor." Sketch didn't say a word to me. He turned to Sheila, who looked like she was ready to go to an exercise class or something, with her sweat suit on and her hair tied up in a colorful scarf and bright red lipstick. You would of thought it was a stranger from across town that was dying, as much consideration as she was paying to the occasion. "Is she dead?" Sketch asked real loud, putting his face right up on her. Sheila though, she wasn't one to just be pushed around and she stood up real tall. "Don't you come walking up on me. I said she was gone. That's all you need to know."

Sketch was like some kind of pit bull got his teeth in someone's arm and ain't letting up. "Is she dead, or is she just gone from here? In an old folks' home or hospital or something?" Now I just told him, but Sketch, he still pretends he doesn't hear me. That's fine with me. I don't know as I want to hang around him anyway. "She's not coming back here," Sheila said with authority, and tried to get past Sketch and into Victoria's place. Sketch jumped to the other side so he was inside the doorway, and she was on the front step, "Is she dead or not?"

"You know, I don't have any problem calling the police."

"No, you have problems acting real. Dammit, where's Miss Cheevers?" Sheila took a minute and looked at Sketch. I swear it was the first time she stood still that entire morning of sweeping and dusting and carrying things upstairs and out to the alleyway trash cans. Sketch was close to six foot tall already, and seemed even sturdier than a few weeks before. His eyes were dark and bold, and they didn't blink or move from Sheila's face, just bored into her like some kind of burning coal. Sheila was frozen for a minute, like she was swimming in the pools of his anger. She tore herself free by quickly telling him where Victoria was. Sketch didn't say another word, just took off running. Not fast, but real easy like, in long loping strides.

It was over an hour before we reached Victoria. On the way I told him I didn't know why he didn't believe me. Sketch, of course, didn't answer, but I couldn't resist pointing out that he did have my good information to go on, without having to get all out of joint with Sheila.

By the time Sketch got to the hospital, Victoria was almost through the passageway. Her skin was translucent; you could see her veins and almost see the blood, not hardly flowing to and from her heart. Now Victoria had stopped talking after Sketch had given her that brooch. Hadn't said a word to anybody, not me, not Sketch, and certainly not Sheila. The doctors thought maybe she was deaf, and Sheila had to admit as to how she really didn't know. Victoria wasn't deaf, just didn't have nothing left to say. Only when they tried to take off her brooch and put on a hospital gown, she grabbed on so tight they had to pry her fingers off. The nurse kept saying, "I've pinned it back on the gown. Look, dear, they're both right here in the top drawer. No one will bother it, dear. And we'll ask the doctor if you can put your own nightdress back on after we do a few tests. All right, dear?"

Sniveling, that's what the nurse was doing, sniveling, talking to her like she didn't have a proper name and was some kind of a child. Now, you tell me, what kind of harm it would do to let Victoria wear her own clothes and keep on her little bit of jewelry. No harm at all, that's what. Well, Victoria she just cried and cried. And me. Well, I must say I let out a few sighs too, because I didn't have a way to help that poor old lady.

When Sketch came in the room, he saw Victoria just lying in the bed, staring at the ceiling. Her skin was dry and cracked and yellow around her eyes. Sketch sat down on the bed next to her, but Victoria, she didn't move her eyes or say a word. I went over to Sketch, "They took her brooch. It's in the drawer here. They won't let her wear her white either. Make her stay in this ugly old hospital gown." Sketch got up and opened the drawer and found the gown and the pin. Then he went over to Victoria with both of them. Then that boy did something that I will forever be grateful for, although at the time I thought it was most improper. He pulled a curtain around the bed so he could have some privacy, and took off Victoria's hospital gown and replaced it with her white dressing gown. All the time he's going, "Excuse me, ma'am," and "Beg your pardon," and trying not to look at her breasts, that are hanging all flat and wrinkled like some empty brown paper bags across her chest. And Victoria she's just flopping here and there, not giving the boy no kind of help, but after a few minutes Sketch has her dressed in her white, with that brooch just shining. By then the nurse came in, and she was getting ready to yell at Sketch, but she saw Victoria start to smile. And when Victoria smiled, and her lips cracked open, I swear this thin stream of light came out with her breath, just a whisper of sun rays out her mouth, hovering in front of her face, and then melting away like morning fog.

Sketch turned to the nurse, "She needs to be in white." The nurse didn't say a word. Victoria reached her hand out towards Sketch's cheek. I think she wanted to say thank you. I know her lips were moving, but nothing was coming out, except this dim light. Then her hand fell onto the bed, and she was gone. Sketch didn't say another word to me or the nurse. Soon as that hand hit the bed, he just took off.

Well, they sure didn't have a funeral for Victoria. Sheila just had her buried in a plot Victoria had paid for decades before, and went on. I thought Victoria would have a last word or two for me, but she didn't, not even a last glance my way. Somehow, I thought when she gave up her body, she'd stay. I guess I'm getting as foolish as she was. Just as well she didn't stay, I say. I mean ever since that fella died she had been being seen more and more, and fussing at me about it. If she kept up like that, folks just might of started hearing me too, and then where would we be? Now, long as I been around, it's not like I don't know how folks be here, and then after awhile they are gone. Not many of us choose to stay. I guess

I just thought somehow she would be one to hang around. I mean I had told her how I figured out how to stay, but she wasn't interested. Started to calling me all kinds of cannibals. Said I was heathen.

It's been over a year since she died. I got to say, I really don't like living in the basement by my lonesome though. First of all, that niece of Victoria's thinks the place is haunted. Now, why would someone want to come and haunt Victoria's place? It's the same as it's been for years, only now Victoria's gone. Sheila is talking about selling the place, I heard her. Now, why she want to go and do a thing like that? Building been in her family for generations. Nigh on a hundred years, you just can't get enough for that kind of knowing a place. But you think that Sheila cares? Not a bit. Talking about moving out to some god-awful place called Hercules. Talking about houses with front yards and garages. Well, there are other things, that's what I say, there are other things that are important. But of course nobody is around to listen to me right now. No one but you, and you don't never talk back, so what's the use in that?

I'm still checking in on Dawa from time to time, but none of them that can hear me choose to, except for Sketch. I tell you, a couple of times he almost answered. Course those that can hear ain't too partial to having my voice in they ears. One time I called out Sketch's name. Well, I called out Jamal, proper like, how Victoria would have done it. Now I know the boy heard me, because Dawa was sitting on the steps that morning just holding her baby and watching the cars go up and down the street. Actually she was nursing that baby. Victoria would have had a fit. Well, Sketch sits down next to her and asks about hearing his name called, but turning around and nobody was there. So, what's that fool know-it-all Dawa have to go and tell him? "You know what they say? You aren't supposed to turn around when somebody calls out your name. Might be a spirit wanting to take your soul."

Now, why would a being like me want to take a soul?

Anyway, Sketch told her how he turned around and nothing happened, just wasn't nobody there. After a while Dawa said, "I guess it's okay to listen, Sketch. But I'd think a few times before I listened too closely to a voice coming from outta nowhere."

Sketch laughed, "Well, I guess it's cool to listen. Long as you don't talk back like the ghost lady. Guess she's happy now, finally got to be a real ghost."

I heard Dawa telling the boy to show Victoria some respect, right before I took off to the beach. I have better things to do than hang around folks talking all ignorant. But ever since that day, even if Sketch does hear me, he doesn't have a word to say. I don't need him to answer me back. I'm thinking about trying to leave this place anyway, maybe go down Los Angeles way. Maybe I'll make it all the way to that Baja California I've heard so much about. Whatever I decide, I know I'm going to stay by the water. It helps me to remember that time before the now days, that time when I had a body in which to swim. Ever since I left my home near the coast, I've always sought out the ocean. Some beings is just supposed to stay near water, and I'm one of them. Victoria, though, insists she was not one of those people. I told her that was crazy. If that was so, why would she of been born so close to the ocean? But Victoria had a way of taking a position and not letting facts get in her way of perceiving a situation. If it wasn't for her learning how to avoid being seen, that, and having me as her guide, the woman would have died years before she did, decades, that's what I say.

Anyway, as I was telling you, I've been out here just over a week, just watching the tides and trying to decide when to move, or even if I should. I used to think I was trapped here, couldn't cross a bridge or get back on a boat or move out of this city. But since Victoria died, it's another thing. I think I could go wherever I pleased. Just as I'm getting ready to make up my mind to move on down the coast, I notice that Dawa and her mother are sitting on the stairs that lead down to the beach. Dawa has her little boy with her. He must be about a year old by now. Cute little boy, hair all windy soft around his head. Real round-faced like Lucille's side of the family, and real noisy like his mother. You know when I told Victoria it was going to be a boy, she started talking about she was looking to see some sandy-haired girl. That woman was as loony as they come. How somebody as deep-toned as Dawa going to have a child with sandy hair. But Victoria never didn't know what she was supposed to know even when it knocked her down. I'm just saying that to say I don't miss her so much as I was used to her being around.

Well, I went up closer to Dawa and Lucille just to see what they were talking. As usual mother and daughter were squabbling.

"That's why I said you should wear pants, Mama. It's always cold by the water." Dawa sighed with exasperation.

"I believe I am clear enough in my mind to dress how I like, Cheryl Ann! Just because you are married and have a baby does not stop you from being my child and not my mother, thank you!" the gray-haired woman responded. "Anyway, I was just commenting on the fact that it was cold. I was not complaining."

"I'm not a child, mama. I haven't been for years. I'm your daughter."

"Child, daughter. Cheryl, it's the same thing. My children are always my children, grown or not."

"Mama, how come you won't call me Dawa, like everybody else?"

"I named you Cheryl Ann—that's your name."

"I grew into another."

"I didn't come out here to bicker with you, child. I'll call you what I will, and how I will."

Dawa sighed, "I'm sorry, Mama."

Now, the two women were sitting on the bottom of the stairs that led down to the shore. Evidently, Lucille had insisted on wearing a dress and stockings, despite her daughter's protest that they were going to have to walk in the soft sand. "I'll take off my shoes if need be, child. If I'm going to see this, I think I'll see it right." Lucille held her wriggling grandson Azania on her lap. He was stretching over her arm trying to pull off his own shoes so he could run down the beach. Dawa reached towards his foot and pulled off the untied stiff-leather training shoes and slipped them into the pockets of her loose jeans. As she leaned over his foot, Azania stretched out his hands and grabbed the one loose dreadlock that had come out of Dawa's ponytail. Lucille softly slapped his hand, and he let loose. Lucille was a contrast to her daughter, with her straight skirt and long wool jacket, her hair coifed in silver and black strands around her head.

The waves were calm, barely hinting at the secrets of the ocean. The fog hovered on the horizon, and the wind slipped moistly under shirt collars and pants cuffs. It was Tuesday morning, so the beach was nearly deserted. A mother ran and caught her toddler in her arms before she waded into the surf. She spun the child around her shoulders and laughed. An older man wearing a mismatched sweat suit tossed a stick towards the ocean as his dog ran out, leaping over the shallow waves to catch it in his mouth and return to shake drops of the sea onto the old man's feet and get ready to leap again. Two young men played frisbee near the shore. Every so often, the frisbee would go over the water, and one would run into the waves, heavy-footed, splashing water and yelling out, shattering the calm of the morning.

Lucille slipped off her short polished black pumps with the tiny spiked heels. Dawa stood up and reached her hand out to her mother. "Come on, Mama, it's time."

The two women walked down the beach towards the retaining wall, with Azania running from one to the other. They didn't speak as they neared the broad expanse of wall that was bright with its yellows, greens, and splashes of red filling in the thick black outlines of Sketch's piece.

"I didn't expect it to be so loud," Lucille said, and moved

closer to the wall. Dawa picked up Azania. "Your cousin Jamal painted this, Azania. He's some kind of hellified artist, isn't he?"

"Cheryl, I don't think you should encourage a baby."

"It's okay, Mama."

Lucille moved to the wall and looked at each detail of the piece. The outlines of Ranger and Victoria had faded in the year since I first saw Sketch draw them. In fact, the horse seemed to stand out more than their pictures. Underneath them was a large fist, solid black, fingers tightly clenched, declaring power, declaring struggle, and, it seemed to me, holding forth the possibility of success. A fist that sturdy couldn't help but get something. At the wrist he had painted his moniker. The "s" was smaller than all the other letters, even though it was first. Its top curve made a brush tip dripping with red into the top of the "K." The "K" looked almost like a man standing taller than all the other letters. The "e" curved around itself like a winking eye with a tear coming from its corner that turned into the dropped "t." The "C" looked like knuckles from a fist, and the "h" was drawn like a flexed arm with the hump a taut biceps. On each knuckle of the hand was a letter of his father's name. The "r" contained a bull's eye in its curl. The "a" was shaped like a broken crack pipe. The upper case "N" stood as a house, while the G looked like the crooked smile his father carried. The "E" looked like three bombs shooting out from a bracket, and the final "r" slid off the fist onto a tombstone. In small neat print, it said, "Ranger and Sketch together forever. R.I.P. Daddy."

Lucille stared at the letters. "Who is that woman over there and what does the horse mean? And what kind of letters are those? Cheryl Lynn, this does not make any sense." Dawa led her mother through each letter, showing her where they started and ended. She didn't say a word about Victoria, didn't even notice that Sketch had painted that brooch in right at her neck. Oh, but she went on pointing out the brush tip, the house, the base pipe. When Dawa reached the eye, Lucille reached out her hand and touched the "T" that formed the tear. "I wanted him to be happy. That's why I let him stay with Ranger and me. Maybe I did wrong. Maybe I should have sided with Mitch and refused him. But how do you refuse your blood? I never could do that... Yes, that boy still doesn't know how to smile enough."

"Mama," Dawa sighed. "It wasn't your fault, he was as happy as he could be with you. But that boy carried a whole lot more heartache than you or I have ever had to carry at so young an age. He saw too much ugly, Mama."

Lucille felt eyes cutting into her skin. She turned and saw a silhouette of a tall thin man moving towards her. He had a certain walk; Lucille frowned up. He loped easy and long just like Ranger. Dawa turned to see what had captured Lucille's attention. "Mama, isn't that Sketch? From back here, I swear he's the image of his father. Jeannine is nowhere to be seen. I thought he was bringing her with him."

Sketch was walking towards them and was smiling ear to ear. As he got closer, Azania turned and ran towards him. Sketch scooped him up and hoisted him to his shoulders. He came close and kissed Dawa. "Hey, Voodoo Auntie! I see you got M'dear out here." Then he put down Azania and gave his grandmother a long hug. He didn't let go of her for a minute as he whispered in her ear, "Thank you for coming. Thank you for coming to see. You know it's been up now for about six months and no one has touched it. Everyone is giving me my props on this one. What you think? I bet Daddy woulda loved it. What you think, M'dear?"

"I see it, but I don't understand. I seriously don't know what to think, boy. How come you can't paint on paper like a regular artist?"

"Cause I'm not regular, M'dear."

"Come on, sit down. Let me show you my piece. This is for Ranger, Ranger and me. So we don't forget, forget him living or forget him dying." Now, who was going to forget that man? Certainly not his mother. That's what I would have said, but why bother, it's not like Sketch was going to listen to me. Too hard-headed to believe his own ears.

Well, Lucille took off her coat, and laid it down on the sand, and then she sat on it. "You know you should have come to the funeral. All these memories are nothing since you didn't come to see him out proper."

Sketch sat down next to his grandmother and picked up her hands. "M'dear, I had had him back for almost a year, and then in those last few months he left again. I just wasn't ready to say goodbye forever."

"And now you are."

Dawa sat next to her mother. "You know, Sketch, he'll come to you in dreams if you let him." I was about to open my mouth and tell Dawa she was wrong, but here comes Sketch talking about, "No. No, you're wrong about that one, Dawa. You can light all the candles you want, but Daddy ain't come back here no kinda way. I don't know where he's on his way to, but I know it's too far to come back, even in dreams." Then the boy moved over to his painting like some kind of a teacher. "Here, let me give you a tour. Now you know the fist is of course black power..."

Dawa and Sketch laughed together for a moment, "Mgawah Black powah," with their inside joke. "I started with the bull's eye because it was hitting his first bull's eye while killing that boy that started to change my father. That's what he told me, and I know it was so..."

Lucille watched as Sketch showed her where each letter was, and told a story for each one. By the time he had reached the "n" she was rocking, rocking in the front row of the funeral parlor where she buried her first born.

Sketch came over and sat next to his grandmother, "Why are you crying, M'dear? He's more alive with this wall, not more dead. Now the sun going to shine on him every sunset until the wind eats this away. And by then, I guess he'll be settled into wherever he had to go."

Lucille looked up at Sketch, "You know, you look just like your father, especially when you smile. You think you could finish that picture of your father that you started before he died?"

Sketch looked at his grandmother and smiled at her, "No, M'dear, I don't think I could. It's as finished as it's supposed to be. But I tell you what, how about I do one of Aunt Cheryl and Ruben and the baby?"

Dawa laughed, "You think Azania is going to sit still for you to draw him? I know you've been spending too much time in the sun."

"Get Mama to take a picture. She said she couldn't get the day off from work, and that's why she didn't come. But if you ask me..."

Dawa looked at Sketch, "Jeannine will come when she's ready."

"If she doesn't come quick, the rollers might have it painted over."

"Then she won't see it, Sketch. We saw it." Dawa gave her nephew a squeeze on the shoulder. "Sketch, why don't you go ahead and take M'dear home? I can tell she's tired, and I want to stay out here a little longer and let Azania play."

"You got it," Sketch said, and helped his grandmother to her feet. The two of them took off. I couldn't resist, so I called out to him, "Your grandmother's got a mess of sand on the back of her coat." I saw both Dawa and Sketch give a start. Dawa called out, "Sketch..." and before she could finish her sentence, or get started really, Sketch says, "M'dear, hold up, let me brush off this sand."

After they left, Dawa just sat there looking at the picture. Azania got restless and scooted out of his mother's lap and started running away. It seemed like Dawa didn't notice, so I called out to her, "Don't you think that boy is getting a little too close to the water?" She got up, calm as you please, and went and got the little boy. I guess she had seen him after all. Then she started digging sand with him, making some kind of a sand building. First she's talking to Azania, telling him that they are building a magic village, and he's just gooing and gurgling and jabbering back at her, as if they are having a real conversation. Then from out of the blue she says, "One time, I heard Victoria telling you to go on when she left. Why didn't you leave?"

Now that was the strangest thing. I've had many people hear me and pretend they don't. I've had people try and humor Victoria, back at the beginning, pretending they heard me, and they didn't hear a word I said. But I hadn't had someone couldn't hear me but talking to me anyway. But Dawa, she went on with just the trace of a quiver in her voice, "I don't know if you are here or anything, or even if you are real. Victoria seemed to think you are. I think you were just a part of her, though. But if it is you, and it was you that's been calling Jamal's name, I'd appreciate it if you'd let him go, and go on to wherever it is you're supposed to be."

Now I start trying to talk to her, tell her I don't mean any harm. Tell her I don't have no hold on Jamal, I just have a little piece of his ear, that's all. I mean, it's not like he's so all fired ready to do anything anybody says he should anyway. If he doesn't pay attention to his grandmother, and only just barely to his stepfather, why in creation is he gonna do a thing I tell him to do? I mean, I even gave him some advice on his painting. Personally, I think it's a little too busy. But did he listen? No! Dawa, she acts like she can't hear a word I say, and now I'm wondering just how long she's been hearing me.

"We're thinking of leaving, Ruben and I. It's a thought. But I'd rather dig in and stay. To tell you the truth I'd like to buy old Victoria's building. I know we can't afford it, but if we sold Mama's place and then rented out Victoria's old apartment, and then had the other unit to rent too, why we might just be able to pull it off. What you think, old haint?"

"I think I'd like that just fine," I say right close to her ear.

"I bet you'd like that just fine. But if I talk Ruben into it, and we pull it off, I really don't want you hanging around. I'm not trying to be unkind; sometimes it just time for a body to move on."

Well, next time I happen onto a body I guess I'll take that into consideration. But tell you true, I really would like to go on down the coast. Dawa started putting Azania's shoes back on his feet, and he was wriggling and squiggling. Then she picks up some sand dollars, and some long strands of yellow green kelp, and some rocks, and holds them with one hand, and holds Azania with the other, as she walks back to the wall with Sketch's work on it. When she gets to the wall, she smooths out the sand right in front and cleans away all the pieces of wood and pebbles and shells of crabs. Then she makes a kind of circle with the kelp and puts the rocks and shells in a pattern, with one rock at each of the directions and the sand dollars, all three of them overlapping arcs at the center. Then she sits right outside the circle with Azania in her lap. He's pulling on her hair, and sticking his fingers in her mouth, and she's taking his hand out of her mouth, and just looking at the wall and the circle real peaceful like. After a while she starts talking.

"You rest in peace, Ranger. If you see Victoria, tell her I'm trying to buy her house. Ask her to send me a blessing."

Then she gets on up, puts Azania on her shoulders, and starts walking towards the stairs and goes up onto the street. I get the feeling she's not coming back to this part of the beach. But I think she's going to stay in the city. That's good. She got a place there. But me, I don't anymore. So I'm going to take off and move down the coast, see if I can find me someone who enjoys a good conversation and is willing to take a little bit of advice from time to time. But for now, I'm just going to watch that sun go down and think about just stretching out to the edge of the horizon, and listen to the waves' breath sizzle into the sand. But I'm leaving this place for sure, soon as I see Dawa and them settled proper as owners of Victoria's place, and say so long to Sketch. Maybe I can even stick just a thought or two inside that hard-head of his before I go.

DEVORAH MAJOR is a poet, novelist and essayist from San Francisco where she works in community programs. In 1989, Juke Box Press published her first book of poetry, *Traveling Women*, a two-poet anthology with Opal Palmer Adisa. Curbstone Press published her second book of poetry, *Street Smarts*, in 1996. Her work has appeared in numerous periodicals and anthologies, including *Callaloo, Zyzzyva, On the Bus, Left Curve* and *Pushcart XII.* Her first novel, *An Open Weave,* was published by Seal Press in 1996 and was awarded the First Novelist Award from the American Library Associations Black Caucus.

CURBSTONE PRESS, INC.

is a non-profit publishing house dedicated to literature that reflects a commitment to social change, with an emphasis on contemporary writing from Latino, Latin American and Vietnamese cultures. Curbstone presents writers who give voice to the unheard in a language that goes beyond denunciation to celebrate, honor and teach. Curbstone builds bridges between its writers and the public – from inner-city to rural areas, colleges to community centers, children to adults. Curbstone seeks out the highest aesthetic expression of the dedication to human rights and intercultural understanding: poetry, testimonies, novels, stories, and children's books.

This mission requires more than just producing books. It requires ensuring that as many people as possible learn about these books and read them. To achieve this, a large portion of Curbstone's schedule is dedicated to arranging tours and programs for its authors, working with public school and university teachers to enrich curricula, reaching out to underserved audiences by donating books and conducting readings and community programs, and promoting discussion in the media. It is only through these combined efforts that literature can truly make a difference.

Curbstone Press, like all non-profit presses, depends on the support of individuals, foundations, and government agencies to bring you, the reader, works of literary merit and social significance which might not find a place in profit-driven publishing channels, and to bring the authors and their books into communities across the country. Our sincere thanks to the many individuals, foundations, and government agencies who support this endeavor: J. Walton Bissell Foundation, Connecticut Commission on the Arts, Connecticut Humanities Council, Daphne Seybolt Culpeper Foundation, Fisher Foundation, Greater Hartford Arts Council, Hartford Courant Foundation, J. M. Kaplan Fund, Eric Mathieu King Fund, John D. and Catherine T. MacArthur Foundation, National Endowment for the Arts, Open Society Institute, Puffin Foundation, and the Woodrow Wilson National Fellowship Foundation.

Please help to support Curbstone's efforts to present the diverse voices and views that make our culture richer. Tax-deductible donations can be made by check or credit card to:

Curbstone Press, 321 Jackson Street, Willimantic, CT 06226
phone: (860) 423-5110 fax: (860) 423-9242
www.curbstone.org

IF YOU WOULD LIKE TO BE A MAJOR SPONSOR OF A CURBSTONE BOOK, PLEASE CONTACT US.